A BIT OF MISCHIEF

At last, Andrew wiped his eyes with the back of his hand and exclaimed, "Why you wily little goose. You've gulled me again."

For the first time in what seemed like ages, but were actually only minutes, Jenny felt it safe to indulge in a sly grin.

"Come along with me, sweetheart," he said gruffly as he pulled her to her feet. "I don't think we'll wait for the tea tray after all."

Jenny couldn't help but note the dangerous glint in his eyes. Stalling for time, she protested, "Oh but, Andrew, I was looking forward to a soothing cup. And, to tell the truth, you look as if you could do with one as well. Could we not wait until—"

Jenny did not get to complete her sentence—much less raise further objections—because at that point Andrew scooped her up and marched from the study. He was halfway up the flight of stairs before a footman bearing the tea tray appeared in the hall below.

Andrew called down to him, "Bring our tea to my wife's sitting room. The viscountess desires a cup before we retire."

"Very good, my lord."

Andrew resumed his rapid pace as he strode down the hall.

"Gracious me. What's your hurry?" Jenny finally worked up the nerve to ask.

Mischief glittered in his dark blue gaze. "Funny you should ask. I, madam, can h̶a̶_____ revenge upon you for dari̶_____ master twice in one evening̶_____

ZEBRA REGENCIES
ARE
THE TALK OF THE TON!

A REFORMED RAKE (4499, $3.99)
by Jeanne Savery

After governess Harriet Cole helped her young charge flee to France — and the designs of a despicable suitor, more trouble soon arrived in the person of a London rake. Sir Frederick Carrington insisted on providing safe escort back to England. Harriet deemed Carrington more dangerous than any band of brigands, but secretly relished matching wits with him. But after being taken in his arms for a tender kiss, she found herself wondering — *could* a lady find love with an irresistible rogue?

A SCANDALOUS PROPOSAL (4504, $4.99)
by Teresa DesJardien

After only two weeks into the London season, Lady Pamela Premington has already received her first offer of marriage. If only it hadn't come from the *ton's* most notorious rake, Lord Marchmont. Pamela had already set her sights on the distinguished Lieutenant Penford, who had the heroism and honor that made him the ideal match. Now she had to keep from falling under the spell of the seductive Lord so she could pursue the man more worthy of her love. Or was he?

A LADY'S CHAMPION (4535, $3.99)
by Janice Bennett

Miss Daphne, art mistress of the Selwood Academy for Young Ladies, greeted the notion of ghosts haunting the academy with skepticism. However, to avoid rumors frightening off students, she found herself turning to Mr. Adrian Carstairs, sent by her uncle to be her "protector" against the "ghosts." Although, Daphne would accept no interference in her life, she *would* accept aid in exposing any spectral spirits. What she never expected was for Adrian to expose the secret wishes of her hidden heart . . .

CHARITY'S GAMBIT (4537, $3.99)
by Marcy Stewart

Charity Abercrombie reluctantly embarks on a London season in hopes of making a suitable match. However she cannot forget the mysterious Dominic Castille — and the kiss they shared — when he fell from a tree as she strolled through the woods. Charity does not know that the dark and dashing captain harbors a dangerous secret that will ensnare them both in its web — leaving Charity to risk certain ruin and losing the man she so passionately loves . . .

Available wherever paperbacks are sold, or order direct from the Publisher. Send cover price plus 50¢ per copy for mailing and handling to Penguin USA, P.O. Box 999, c/o Dept. 17109, Bergenfield, NJ 07621. Residents of New York and Tennessee must include sales tax. DO NOT SEND CASH.

The Golden Swan

Phylis Warady

ZEBRA BOOKS
KENSINGTON PUBLISHING CORP.

ZEBRA BOOKS are published by

Kensington Publishing Corp.
475 Park Avenue South
New York, NY 10016

Zebra and the Z logo Reg. U.S. Pat. & TM Off.

First Printing: May, 1994

Printed in the United States of America

One

1810 . . .

A knock on the library door caused Aubrey Halpern, the 7th Marquess of Buxton, to run his hand through his bushy thatch of coarse iron gray hair. He'd have thought that Andrew, now eight and twenty, would've had sense enough not to get entangled in such an imbroglio. By Jove, he did not look forward to the upcoming interview. Yet he owed it to a long line of illustrious ancestors to rescue his son and heir from the brink of disaster.

With a martyred sigh, the marquess returned the miniature of Andrew as a child to its accustomed place on his desk. Disgruntled though he was, there was no question in his mind that he loved his son fiercely.

"Come," he called in a gruff voice.

Andrew Halpern, Viscount Temple, strode into the room. He held a riding crop in his left hand and tapped it intermittently against his thigh. The air crackled with his vibrant energy.

"Excuse me, Pater, for appearing before you in

all my dirt, but you did say it was urgent, did you not?"

The marquess discerned the subtle edge underlying his son's baritone drawl that made a mockery of the foppish turn of phrase Andrew had assumed—no doubt in the hope that it would ignite his father's lamentable hair-trigger temper. However, Andrew would catch cold at that, since Buxton had himself well in hand. Indeed, after a moment's reflection, he decided the edge in his offspring's voice could be attributed to Andrew's resentment of being summoned to Devon while the London Season was in full swing.

Awake to his son's monkey tricks, the marquess embarked on a leisurely inspection of the younger man's attire—an exercise that in the past had caused him to gnash his teeth in impotent fury. Today, however, his eyes twinkled at the lengths his son was willing to go to irritate him. Indeed, his offspring was the epitome of sartorial distinction in a brown corduroy riding coat tailored to set off broad shoulders to a nicety, tan breeches, and dusty cordovan boots, each sporting a braided gold tassel.

"Rubbish! I've never been one to stand on ceremony here at Halpern Abbey."

Andrew's lips twitched. "In that case, sir, perhaps you won't object if I pour myself a drop of brandy to clear the road dust from my throat?"

"By all means, help yourself."

Watching his son pour the amber potation into a glass, the marquess wished they understood each other better. Not only didn't they think alike, their temperaments were as different as chalk and cheese. By George, they didn't even look like each other.

Short and stocky best described the marquess, whereas Andrew possessed a wiry frame and topped his father's height by several inches. Furthermore, while the marquess had a tendency to plod, his son moved with the fluid grace of a sleek tomcat.

Buxton held no illusions in regard to his own appearance. His was a homely, rubicund phiz, faintly reminiscent of a pugnacious pug. Not that he envied born beauties. To depend upon physical beauty alone was tantamount to standing on quicksand and expecting the ground beneath you not to give way.

Indeed, the marquess almost wished Andrew had inherited his homeliness. If he had, he was convinced his son wouldn't be presently involved in a wretched scandal that threatened to end his career. But Andrew took after his mother in looks. And perhaps in moral laxity as well.

Buxton clenched his hands into fists. Of course, Andrew could not help it, that his handsome features might have been carved from marble by Michelangelo. But, by God, no son of his would become a hardened profligate so long as he had anything to say about it. And he had plenty to say as Andrew would soon learn to his sorrow.

On the other hand, he didn't want to be too

hard on him either. Frowning, the marquess opened his fists and shook his hands to alleviate the cramps caused by clenching them so tightly. While curbing his son's amorous adventures was important, he had no desire to turn Andrew into a lap dog.

Buxton's brow cleared. Lap dog, indeed. The very notion was so ridiculous, it prompted a bark of laughter.

"Something amuses you, Pater? Perhaps you'd care to share it?"

"Nothing of moment," he said gruffly.

His handsome cub's back was turned as he strode to the sideboard. The marquess preferred to wait until his son faced him before they got into it.

Ridding himself of his empty glass, Andrew sketched a mock bow. "Sir, I await your pleasure."

The marquess stared straight into the viscount's dark blue eyes. "I'm disappointed in you, son. To be branded an adulterer once this divorce case reaches Parliament is infamous. Tell me, are Quinlan's accusations justified?"

The younger man ran a finger beneath a suddenly too-tight neckcloth. "I fear so."

"Crazy young jackanapes! How dare you drag the family name through the mud!"

Andrew took a vicious swipe at his thigh with his riding crop. "Go ahead and vent your spleen, sir, if it makes you feel any better. Silly of me to expect my father might be more understanding."

The marquess struggled to contain his irritation. "Spare me your sarcasm, if you please. What did Castlereagh have to say?"

"Plenty. After singeing my ears, he placed me on indefinite leave."

"Well there you are!" Buxton wagged his index finger at his son. "If you don't have a care, you'll scuttle a brilliant career in the foreign service."

"No need to fly into the boughs, sir. I promise to be more circumspect in the future. It's just that Lady Quinlan was such a tempting morsel. Still, who'd suspect her husband would cut up so stiff?"

Up to now, the marquess had managed to keep a lid on his temper, but Andrew's eagerness to shift responsibility blew it sky high. "By damn, it's time you stop letting your passions rule you. It's time you took a wife and settled down."

The hand that held the riding crop froze in midair. "A wife, sir? I'm only eight and twenty. Plenty of time for that later on."

"Not later on. Now. I wish you to be wed immediately."

"Impossible! With all due respect, until the unsavory details of the Quinlan divorce case die down, I'm *persona non grata* in the eyes of society. Next Season will be soon enough to look the field over and select a bride."

The marquess spoke through gritted teeth. "There will be no year's grace. You have one week to procure a special license and marry the young woman I've chosen for you."

"See here, sir. I won't be forced to wed against my wishes."

"Confound it! You will do as you're told," roared the marquess, then added in a more reasonable tone, "Marriage and temporary retirement in the country is the only way to salvage your career. I don't mean to brag, but I'm not without influence. While you rusticate, I shall exert myself to hush up the more unsavory aspects of this unfortunate divorce case."

"Sir, I don't wish you to think I don't appreciate your efforts on my behalf. But marriage is so . . . permanent."

"Exactly so! To be plain, it's time you stopped flitting from flower to flower and took a wife. Mark my words, it'll be the making of you."

The marquess ventured a sly peek at his son. Andrew looked decidedly glum.

"This bride you've hand-picked, do I know her?"

"I doubt it. You're here at the Abbey so seldom. She's lived all her life in Sticklepath. Kept house for her father who died last year leaving her virtually penniless."

Andrew gave a scornful laugh. "This is rich. You, sir, who are forever prosing about what's due the family name, wish me to marry a nobody, a penniless waif?"

The marquess bristled. "Jenny may be an orphan, but her family tree is unexceptional. Her mother was the daughter of a baron. She married Curtis Shaw, youngest son of the Earl of Leeds."

Andrew, the marquess reflected, seemed to need an inordinate amount of time to digest his future wife's lineage. Oh well. Let him search high and low. He'd find nothing in her pedigree to take exception to.

"How old is she?"

"Seventeen."

"Seventeen? Really, Pater, must you pair me up with some chit fresh from the schoolroom?"

The expression in marquess's eyes hardened. "Better a naive, unsophisticated wife than a worldly wanton."

Andrew responded with a harsh laugh. "Point taken, sir, but I'm a career diplomat. I need a wife whose social skills will help me advance—not some green country miss."

"I beg to differ. A green country miss is exactly what you need to establish roots. Any social skills she lacks can be taught. But I have not finished cataloging my list of demands."

Andrew sketched a mock bow. "By all means continue. I'm all ears."

"Very well. Not only will you marry Jenny, you will reside with her in the country until she delivers your heir."

"Ho! I begin to understand. You don't care a fig for my career. You don't care if both the waif and I are miserable together so long as we produce an heir."

"Precisely. In exchange for your compliance, I'll do my utmost to scotch the scandal that threatens to put a period to your usefulness in the diplomatic service. This may well be your last chance to put things right. So tell me, sir, do you accept my proposal or not?"

Andrew released a tortured sigh. "It appears I've no other choice."

Inside a small, nondescript bungalow situated on the outskirts of Sticklepath, the pungent odor of singed hair wafted to Jenny Shaw's small, straight nose.

"Ouch!" she cried, glaring at the abigail. "Have a care with that curling iron, Nell."

"I be ever so sorry, miss. Did I burn your scalp?"

"No, just my hair."

Jenny gazed into the mirror at her now hopelessly frizzed bangs. Why must she be plagued with flyaway tresses that had no fullness? Indeed, both its white-blond color and its fluffy texture put her in mind of a newborn duckling. And now the maid had managed to singe her hair.

A deep sigh escaped. She wished Nell could wave a magic wand and make her look pretty. Not very realistic, she supposed, but after all it was her wedding day.

Jenny wished she didn't feel so on edge. Still who wouldn't be nervous? In less than an hour she would wed a man she'd never laid eyes on before.

Could she actually go through with this? Jenny asked herself when informed by Nell that the conveyance sent by Lord Buxton stood at the front door. Indeed, her knees wobbled so badly, she wasn't sure her nether limbs were capable of supporting her as far as the waiting coach, let alone down the aisle.

Sad-eyed, Jenny darted glances about the bed-chamber she'd occupied as far back as she could remember. A year ago, she'd said goodbye to Papa. Now she took a moment to say goodbye to familiar objects she suspected she'd never see again. True, the wallpaper was peeling, the curtains threadbare, and the carpet faded. Yet it was her home, and she hated to leave.

Not that she had any other choice, she acknowledged as a liveried footman assisted her into the coach. Truly, she felt like a pawn subject to the whim of her fatherly benefactor. Jenny continued to brood as the coachman gave the horses the office to start. Think of it! Up until a few days past, her heart had swelled with gratitude whenever she recalled how Lord Buxton had insisted she stay on in the bungalow rent free during her year of mourning.

She let out a great sigh. How naive could she be? She should have known there'd be a price exacted in exchange for the marquess's many kindnesses.

Her understandable pique at his lordship's recent high-handedness notwithstanding, when the conveyance rolled to a stop at the church entrance, Jenny was relieved to spot Lord Buxton's homely face. As he helped her alight, he brusquely swept aside her thanks for sending his coach to collect her. As always, she found the marquess's manner bracing. Not that she minded. Given a choice, she preferred gruff honesty to reticence, and if his son were anything like him, Jenny was persuaded they'd rub along well together as a married couple.

Nonetheless, all manner of questions plagued her. For example, why did the marquess think it necessary to choose a bride for his only son? No one had asked her opinion, of course, but Jenny felt that it would have made better sense to leave the choice of a wife up to Lord Temple. He was the person who'd have to live with the consequences.

"My dear, Andrew wishes a private word with you."

"Before the ceremony?" she squeaked.

Merciful heavens! Suppose the viscount took one look at her and refused to marry someone so plain? Should he reject her, her pride would no longer permit her to stay on in the bungalow. But where would she go?

Papa had barely eked out a living as a translator, and his death had rendered her a pauper. True, her grandfather was the Earl of Leeds, but unfortunately when Curtis Shaw had wed penniless Minnie Potter instead of the heiress his father had picked out for his youngest son, the earl had been so infuriated he'd disinherited him. Thus, not only was Jenny a pauper with no trade or marketable skills, she had no family to turn to.

Jenny experienced a rush of pure terror at the magnitude of the step she was about to take. The marquess must have noticed the slight tremor in the hand she rested upon his sleeve, for he squeezed it gently.

"Ah, here's the curate to escort you to the vestry, where you two lovebirds may converse in private."

Lovebirds? No description was less apt, Jenny thought. If only she weren't so . . . so ugly.

The marquess issued her a reassuring smile. "Run along, my dear. Andrew promises to keep you only a moment. I'll be here when you return. I have the honor of escorting you down the aisle."

Jenny trudged after the clergyman as if approaching her doom. Presently the hinges squeaked as the door to the vestry swung open and the curate led her inside. She peered curiously into the murkiness but failed to catch so much as a glimpse of the bridegroom.

"My lord, I'll be back in ten minutes to collect Miss Shaw. Mind, the vicar's a high stickler for punctuality."

As the door squeaked to a close behind her, Jenny drifted toward the soft glow of candlelight emanating from a candelabrum resting upon a lacquered table. But before she reached her destination, a tall lanky gentleman stepped out of the shadows. Jenny froze, awe-struck.

If she were limited to a single word to describe her future husband, she'd choose *elegant*. Indeed, his pin-striped trousers and dark blue serge coat were so fine, they put her own attire to shame.

The viscount acknowledged her with a cool nod, then stood motionless as if he sensed she needed time to adjust to his presence. His face and figure were so perfectly wrought, Jenny wished she'd brought her sketch pad. Even more compelling was a wanton impulse to run her hands through the raven ringlets that softened the chiseled contours of his face. Never had she seen such a beautiful specimen of manly grace. Adonis come to life!

Still in all, there was something beyond physical beauty that captured her fancy. Something indefinable about this man drew her with a magnetic power she found almost impossible to resist. At first, this unknown quality proved elusive. However, once Jenny redoubled her efforts, she realized that he was the exact opposite of her reclusive, scholarly father. Of course she'd loved Papa, but there was no denying she'd resented his ability to lapse into a brown study whenever some household crisis loomed, leaving Jenny to resolve it as best she could. Thus it was her prospective bridegroom's vitality, his *joie de vivre*, that tugged at her heartstrings.

A tender smile spread across her face only to be swiftly superseded by a vaguely troubled expression. Most emphatically, she did not believe in love at first sight. She tried to tell herself there was no such thing. Her heart paid no heed. It skipped, then pulsed faster.

"You're hugging the shadows. Step into the light."

Jenny took a deep breath and stepped forward.

"Good lord, ma'am, you can't mean to be wed

wearing black. Father gave me to understand you were out of mourning."

Jenny chewed on her lower lip. While dark colors helped slenderize her full figure, black was by no means her best color. Standing alongside him at the altar, she'd look like a veritable dowd. "The year is up, but I wasn't given enough time to order a more suitable gown."

She hadn't had the funds either, but she was too proud to admit it. Her heart quaked when he peered at her through his quizzing glass. She was almost certain he despised what he saw, but couldn't be absolutely sure since his partially lowered eyelids made it difficult to read his expression. When he dropped his quizzing glass, she saw that his eyes were dark blue and fringed with thick, spiky black lashes. But that was neither here nor there, she told herself crossly.

Jenny squared her shoulders. "So I donned my black silk. It's my best."

"I see," he drawled, a hint of boredom marring the rich timbre of his baritone voice. "I assume Father informed you I wished a word with you before the ceremony."

Her chin came up. *She would not be intimidated.* "As a matter of fact, there are certain matters I wish to discuss as well."

Though he took pains to mask it, the rigid set of his shoulders indicated that the viscount had mistakenly assumed that, because she was plain, she'd allow him to ride roughshod over her. Well, the sooner she disabused him of such a bacon-brained notion the better!

He gave a mock bow. "Madam, you have the floor."

She countered with a mock curtsy. "Indeed, my lord, you are all consideration. I merely wish to explain my reasons for acceding to your father's scheme."

Quite by chance, she caught a clear glimpse into his eyes. The animosity she saw there chilled to the marrow.

"Madam, I neither know nor care why you've consented to wed a perfect stranger. For my part, I have no choice but to marry at once."

What a facer! The viscount was even more reluctant than she to go through with the ceremony. If those were his sentiments, she couldn't help but wonder why he'd agreed to the proposed loveless union.

"But before we take that irrevocable step," Andrew Halpern continued, "I wish to be sure you understand the terms. Did my father explain that I only agree to cohabitate with you until you produce an heir?"

How unkind of him to remind her that her part in this unfolding drama was tantamount to that of a brood mare. Whether it was his intention or not, the reminder cast a pall on the day. The last of Jenny's girlish dreams crumbled in the face of his callow disregard for her feelings. Ice cold, her teeth began to chatter. Not only did the bridegroom look like a Greek god chipped from marble, his nature was equally chilly.

Jenny stiffened her spine. She refused to be crushed by his cynicism. "Yes, he did."

"Splendid. Kindly oblige me by repeating what he said."

"He explained ours was to be a marriage of convenience and that once I've borne you a son, we're both free to pursue separate lives."

"And you agreed to this?"

"Indeed, my lord, in common with you, I have no other choice."

Unnerved by his supercilious stare, Jenny lowered her gaze and commenced drawing circles with the toe of one satin slipper. The fact that Andrew Halpern was cleverly disguised as a handsome prince didn't fool her for a minute.

The curate's reappearance broke the unbearable tension. As Jenny fell in behind him, it galled her to think that she must marry such a toad.

Nonetheless, she forced herself to return the smile the marquess awarded her once she rejoined him in the foyer. Though, thanks to the bridegroom, her wedding day was ruined, there was no point in making her future father-in-law unhappy.

Jenny kept in step with the organ music as she glided down the aisle on the marquess's arm. She spoke her vows in a clear, sweet voice, scarcely aware of what she said or did. Indeed, her spirits were so overset that ever afterward, her memory of the actual ceremony remained hazy.

Two

His demeanor pensive, Andrew Halpern refolded the *London Times* and set it beside his plate. He'd waded through the parliamentary reports, court, shipping, and foreign news, savoring every tidbit. But now that he had, time would hang heavy on his hands until tomorrow morning, when the entire process would repeat itself. In the four-odd months he and Jenny had resided in Leicestershire, the ritual never changed—nor for that matter did his resentment that he was trapped here for God only knew how long.

The problem with backwater communities was not only did the London papers arrive several days late, but the bucolic settings lacked excitement—an ingredient Andrew craved. God, how he missed embassy life! Stuck here at his father's hunting box, he missed the splendor of foreign courts and the sophisticated beauties that adorned them, missed the cut and thrust of verbal fencing that challenged to the hilt his diplomatic skills, missed the intrigues hatched behind the scenes that were such a pleasure to thwart. Of course he missed it. It was where he thrived.

It was where he belonged. Nowhere else was life so exciting.

Jenny breezed into the breakfast room. Andrew was amused by her slapdash entrance. What it lacked in polish, it made up for in enthusiasm.

"Good morning, sprite."

She arched an eyebrow so pale against her smooth ivory skin it was barely discernible. "You're dressed in riding clothes. Shall I change into my habit?"

For once, Andrew's glib tongue failed him. He'd risen earlier than usual on purpose. With dismay, he watched the animation that enlivened Jenny's features dim. He felt like an ogre.

"You don't wish company?"

"It's not that. I've business in Melton Mowbray."

"I see. No doubt I'd slow you down."

Andrew regarded her slumped shoulders with a twinge of guilt as she made her selection from the variety of dishes on the sideboard. She'd looked so happy, so carefree when she'd entered the room.

Jenny carried her plate to the table and seated herself. As she reached for her serviette, she spotted the wrapped gift beside her place setting. Her face lit up and she gave a squeal of delight. The expression in Andrew's eyes softened. His country-bred wife was really very sweet. At times like this, even her coltish clumsiness seemed endearing.

"For me?"

"You're eighteen today, are you not?"

"Yes. I wasn't sure you'd remember."

Grinning, he shook his head. "With all the hints you've dropped? Happy birthday, my dear."

She tore into the wrapping paper like an avid field hand tackling ripe wheat with a scythe. Andrew couldn't help but smile at her eagerness. But once she opened the lid of the slender box and peeked inside, she gazed at him uncertainly.

"A diamond bracelet?"

"Excellent guess," he quipped as he lifted it from the slender box. "Hold out your wrist. I'll do the honors."

She stared at him from wide-set hazel eyes flecked with gold. As if mesmerized, she slowly extended her arm.

Once the bracelet circled her wrist, he cautioned, "This clasp is tricky. Make sure it's properly fastened whenever you wear it."

"Living so quietly, I hardly think I'll have much occasion." She thrust out her arm. "Undo it, if you please."

Her response unsettled him. The bracelet had set him back a pretty penny. Any of the beauties he'd courted in the past would have snapped it up in a minute. Not so Jenny. Clearly she considered it a useless trinket. As he returned the bracelet to its box, he found himself both disgruntled and intrigued by her lack of avarice.

The muted chimes of a clock tolled the hour. Andrew rose. "Is there anything I can bring you from Melton? More charcoal pencils? Another sketch pad?"

"Both would be nice. And a box of pastels if it's not too dear."

"Oh, I think my funds will stretch that far."

Though eager to be off, he couldn't bear to leave her looking so woeful. "I'll be back by noon. How does a picnic by the brook sound?"

Jenny responded by jumping to her feet and awarding him a spontaneous hug. Andrew swallowed the suspicious lump in his throat as he gently disentangled himself from her embrace.

"Eat your breakfast, sprite, before it gets cold," he said, then made good his escape before his reckless tongue promised the moon.

Riding to town, his thoughts continued to revolve around Jenny. Plain or no, there were aspects to her personality that pleased him. Sunny-natured, she was easy to talk to whenever he desired to air some grievance or express an opinion, yet restful to be around when he was engaged in silent contemplation.

However, by far the most surprising aspect of their relationship was the passion he'd awakened in his bride on their wedding night. Andrew's brow puckered. Truth be told, the depth of her emotional response during conjugal intimacy both delighted and disturbed. Her unguarded openness might be part of her charm, but it also rendered her vulnerable. He didn't want to hurt her if he could avoid it and decided to be careful of what he said and did. To allow himself to be drawn too close to her steady glow would be most unwise. Drawing too close to anyone was risky.

He'd made that mistake as a child with his
mother, and the bitterness he'd reaped when
she'd deserted him without a backward glance
had taught him a valuable lesson.

To be sure, Jenny was nothing like his mother.
Actually she was very . . . giving. But as much
as she delighted him here in Leicester, she'd
never shine in London society or in the glittering
diplomatic world where he excelled. He must
guard against losing his perspective. His time
with Jenny was but a temporary idyll, and while
he had every intention of enjoying their interval
together, he must take care not to get caught in
her artless snare.

A rabbit skittered across the road, causing his
mount to rear. It took all of his concentration to
regain control of the prancing horse, and once
he had, his train of thought veered off in an
entirely different direction.

Whatever had possessed him to give his country-bred wife a diamond bracelet? To someone as
unsophisticated as Jenny, it was a perfectly useless
gift. Happily, it wasn't too late to make amends.
He could buy her something else in town. But
what? When he tried to think of a more appro-
priate present, he drew a blank.

Fortunately just before he reached the outskirts
of Melton Mowbray, he espied a cluster of hearts-
ease growing by the wayside that caused him to
recollect Jenny's fondness for wildflowers. Indeed,
her sketchbooks were crammed with examples of
local blooms drawn during their frequent coun-

tryside rambles. Surprisingly her sketches showed considerable talent. Although untutored in botany until he'd awakened her interest, her mind was like a sponge eager to soak up whatever information she could glean on that subject. His brow cleared as he hit upon the perfect gift for Jenny.

Smiling absent-mindedly, Andrew watched Jenny sip her customary before-dinner glass of sherry. Conscious that his earlier present had fallen flat, he was eager to make amends. Consequently he made sure to compliment her on her rose silk evening gown—one of several he'd commissioned the first week of their honeymoon to replace her dowdy wardrobe of unrelieved black. Though the most skillful of seamstresses would have difficulty showing off his wife's figure to advantage, at least the delicate rose shade of her gown called attention to her ivory complexion.

Truth be told, Andrew was on pins and needles by the time he seated her at the dining-room table. The comical expression on Jenny's face when she noticed a package wrapped in silver paper beside her plate made him chuckle.

"Another gift?"

"So it seems."

Her eyes grew soft and luminous. "You'll spoil me."

Andrew felt a curious constriction in the vicinity of his heart. His smile slipped a fraction. "Open it," he commanded tersely.

Jenny didn't wait to be told twice. She tore into the silver paper, and it fell unheeded to the floor. Andrew would sooner drink hemlock than admit it, but he loved to watch the play of emotions on her expressive face. Thus, when he caught a gleam of genuine pleasure in her gaze, he felt immeasurably rewarded.

"Why, it's a book!"

"Fancy that," he teased, then added in a more serious vein, "You displayed such an avid interest in botany, I thought you might enjoy owning Phillip Miller's *Gardening Kalendar.*"

Jenny's eyes shone like rare jewels. "Indeed, my lord, it's a capital gift. Thank you."

He grinned, for once in perfect charity with his country wife. "You're welcome, sprite."

Andrew woke to the patter of soft rain upon the hunting box's gambrel roof. He glanced out the window at the overcast sky and then at the Avignon clock resting upon the mantelpiece.

A little past nine. Later than he usually rose. Reluctant to leave his warm cocoon, he decided to test the waters by poking a toe out from under the bedclothes.

"Devil a bit!" he exclaimed as he yanked his toe back beneath the covers. "It's nippy out there."

Andrew frowned. For the first time, he regretted his edict forbidding any of the staff to enter their bedchamber each morning until summoned.

Grumbling, he bounded out of bed. Reaching the hearth, he hunkered down on his haunches. Stirring the embers, he added coal, a piece at a time, to the dying fire until he'd finally coaxed forth a cheerful blaze.

Arising, he did a few knee bends to stimulate circulation cut off by his prolonged crouch. A scant minute later, he succumbed to temptation and crawled back into bed. As the warmth he craved seeped into his body, he grinned. A day like this did not lend itself to dashing about. It was a day to linger in the cozy warmth of one's bed. Especially when that bed contained one's very own wife.

A look of unholy glee cropped into his dark blue eyes. To take it a step further, it was a day tailor-made for lovemaking.

As though on cue, Jenny stirred. Propping himself up on one elbow, he watched the gentle rise and fall of her chest and realized she still dozed. Asleep, she looked so vulnerable it triggered his protective instincts, and despite his burgeoning desire, he decided the only honorable course was to bide his time until she woke.

Then without warning, Jenny snuggled against him. Andrew groaned, and thoroughly aroused by her innocent assault, his control snapped. Abandoning his self-imposed role of chivalrous knight, he gathered her close to his hard lean body and proceeded to touch and stroke her until she was equally intoxicated.

Awash in a world of sensuality, Jenny dreamt

she was scaling the face of a rocky cliff, and just when she'd begun to doubt she'd ever reach the crest, her universe exploded into a million pieces. For a seeming eon, she felt enveloped in a sensuous glow, though marginally aware that it would soon end.

Jenny opened her eyes and fixed her gaze upon her husband. Andrew's face wore a devilish grin. "Tired of playing possum? Hmm?"

"No such thing!" She frowned. "You woke me up."

His eyes danced. "Guilty as charged. Do you realize 'tis almost ten o'clock?"

Jenny's eyes grew round as saucers. "Surely you jest."

He shook his head. "Listen to the rain."

Awareness of the soft patter of raindrops on the roof overhead seeped into her consciousness. Feeling safe and cherished, she observed, "There's something about soft rainfall that makes one a trifle lazy, is there not?"

"Exactly so!" Andrew nibbled on her earlobe, then observed in a husky whisper, "Sweetheart, you might be late to rise, but some parts of you are by no means lethargic. So would you mind very much if we repeat the process?"

Her eyes had closed to better savor the delicious sensations Andrew's lips evoked as he trailed gossamer kisses the length of her jawbone. Startled by his seductive tone, they flew open.

"Repeat the process? Whatever do you mean?"

Andrew answered with a rakish grin that melted

Jenny's insides. Her rosy blush confirmed the exact instant the gist of his message sunk in.

"Now? In the daylight?"

"Yes. Shocking, am I not?"

"Very," she agreed dryly.

His eyes twinkled. "Sweetheart, you are in for a treat. Come to me, my dearest shrinking violet, and I'll show you what I mean."

That evening found Jenny seated at her dressing table while Dora, the young servant assigned to be her personal maid, did her hair. Normally she enjoyed watching the girl's clever fingers impose a semblance of order on her wispy locks.

Not this time though. Because, shameless hussy that she was, after spending almost the entire day in bed with her husband, she dared not watch for fear she'd inadvertently catch the abigail's eye and see censure therein.

"M'lady, please stand up so I can be certain the hem of your gown be even."

Rising, she turned slowly while the abigail concentrated her gaze upon the hemline of the amber jaconet dinner dress. Finally, having come full circle, Jenny began to tap her slippered foot.

"Dora, my patience is not infinite. How much longer?"

"Not another second." Dora smiled. "The hem be straight."

After dismissing her maid, Jenny made her way to Andrew's study, where she learned he'd already poured her sherry. As he handed it to her, their fingertips touched. As a jolt of sensual current passed between them, her pupils darkened to molten gold. Swiftly she lowered her gaze, not wanting him to see her tender regard reflected in her eyes. Since Andrew did not love her, such a revelation could only embarrass them both.

Jenny drew a deep, fortifying breath, knowing it was pointless to wish for the impossible. At least she and Andrew were on cordial terms. She grinned. Indeed, it would be fair to say they were on *more* than cordial terms, sensually speaking.

In the dining room, he seated her to his immediate right. Her flush deepened as she recalled what a devilish time she'd had persuading Andrew that they ought to dress for dinner. Her husband could be quite stubborn, so when he'd insisted breakfast and lunch be brought to their bedchamber, she'd raised no objection. But when he'd wanted to order the servants to serve dinner there, too, Jenny had balked.

So, as usual, they were eating their meal off Meissen china in the dining room. Thank goodness! For if Andrew had gotten his way, heaven only knew what the servants would think of her conduct, honeymoon or no!

At the meal's conclusion, Andrew instructed the butler to convey his compliments to the cook, then escorted Jenny into his study.

Jenny seated herself in her favorite upholstered chair and picked up her sketch pad. When they'd first married, Andrew had discouraged her from so much as crossing the threshold of the room he regarded as his private sanctuary. But gradually they'd reached a compromise. Daytimes still remained sacrosanct. However, evenings had evolved into a time of companionship, and he always welcomed her presence here before and after dinner.

Andrew sauntered over to the chessboard, picked up a castle, examined it, set it down and strode off. Normally Jenny looked forward to spending the evening with him, but tonight he couldn't seem to settle down. Troubled by his restlessness, she watched him pace back and forth until she could hold her tongue no longer.

"My lord, watching you makes me dizzy. For heaven's sake, alight somewhere before you wear a hole in the carpet."

Andrew halted in mid-stride. Looking astonished, then amused, he bowed and said, "Your wish is my command, madam."

Observing him lean against the mantelpiece as if he didn't have a care in the world, Jenny smelled a rat. She was too sensitively attuned to her husband not to realize that, despite his casual pose, he was having a terrible time controlling his fidgets. It seemed she had a caged panther on her hands. One that craved freedom to roam. Perhaps, she reasoned, Andrew had had a surfeit of her company for one day and desired privacy.

"Don't be bashful," Jenny advised. "If you'd like me to leave, say so."

Andrew threw her a wicked grin. "No such

thing! I was just wondering how to occupy ourselves until the tea tray appears. Other than making love here in the study, of course."

Jenny turned crimson. "Really, sir, you promised to behave yourself."

"Am I to take it you're not interested?" he crooned.

"Of a certainty!" she snapped.

"Pity that." His eyes held a devilish twinkle. "Cards then? Or do you play?"

"Only whist. And it requires another couple."

So his wife was not totally devoid of social skills, thought Andrew. He tucked this nugget away to be examined later. However, he still had a problem since he'd promised to keep his hands to himself until bedtime. But in order to do that, he needed a diversion engrossing enough to distract him.

He scanned the room as if it might hold the answer to his dilemma. His eyes halted when they reached the chess table.

"I don't suppose you play chess, do you?"

Expression shy, Jenny swallowed twice and confessed, "As a matter of fact, I used to play with my father."

"Well, if that don't beat the Dutch!" Andrew stared at her thoughtfully. "What other hidden talents do you have tucked up your sleeve, hmm?"

Flustered, she said, "None whatsoever, I do assure you. As to my chess game, I fear I'm woefully out of practice."

Andrew awarded her a measured look. "I'm a bit rusty myself. Still, I want to be fair. So rather than flip a coin to see who goes first, you take the white."

Three

Andrew made a cursory inspection of the chessboard before moving his rook a space forward. In the first fifteen minutes of play, he'd concluded Jenny was no match for him and had mapped out a strategy to prolong the game. Because, while he'd have enjoyed a genuine challenge, he was willing to settle for a chance to promote a closer relationship between them.

"Check," Jenny said softly.

"Check? What the deuce are you talking about?"

"You walked into my trap."

"The devil you say!"

Jenny shrugged. "See for yourself."

He took a closer look at the chessboard. Curse it! He could see no way out. That'd teach him not to be so complacent. By underestimating his opponent's abilities, he'd laid the groundwork for his own defeat.

Unless of course her win was based on pure luck. To test his theory, Andrew deliberately placed his king in jeopardy. Jenny quickly moved her chessman in for the kill.

"Checkmate," she cried.

His dark blue eyes narrowed. By George, he'd been gulled. Andrew regarded his unpresupposing wife with dawning respect. Clearly she was more intelligent than he'd realized.

"Another game?"

"If you wish. But are you certain you can withstand two defeats in a row?" Jenny asked sweetly.

Andrew had a devil of a time stopping himself from gnashing his teeth. The last thing he wanted was to wind up on the losing end again. But if his experience in the diplomatic service had taught him nothing else, it had taught him the value of keeping his temper in check and his mind properly focused.

Bristling with renewed confidence, he could hardly wait for the play to commence. The sooner it did, the sooner he could trounce her soundly. However, twenty minutes into the match, his mood was no longer sanguine. They were so evenly matched, it was impossible to predict who'd emerge victorious. Yet, a second defeat on his part was not to be tolerated. There had to be something he could do to tip the scales in his favor.

He admired his wife's long tapered fingers as they closed about a black knight. During the wedding ceremony, her gloves had hidden her badly chapped hands. However, now that she could rely on servants to perform most of the menial tasks, her hands were snowy white and soft to the touch.

As he watched Jenny move her black knight

three spaces, his eyes gleamed with sudden inspiration. And once she let go of the chess piece, he reached across the game table and took hold of her hand.

Jenny, who was no fool, cast him a suspicious glance and asked, "Whatever are you about?"

Assuming a look of bland innocence, he said soothingly, "Nothing diabolical, I assure you. I'm merely yielding to a whimsical urge to hold hands."

Even as he spoke, he began to trace tiny circles upon the sensitive skin at the base of her wrist. The sensation created by his gossamer touch heated Jenny's blood. But more importantly, the assault on her senses broke her concentration.

"Dashed pretty hands. So soft, so touchable," Andrew murmured as he surreptitiously repositioned one of his bishops.

And to further insure that her emotions remained in turmoil, he deliberately touched the tip of his tongue to the sensitized skin where he'd been drawing erotic circles with his thumb. A flood tide of scalding current rushed along Jenny's skin. And even though she was quick to snatch back her hand, her heightened awareness of her husband's virile presence made it difficult to keep her mind on the game in progress.

Indeed, she found herself in a quandary. His seductive voice called to her. On the other hand, she deemed it important to win the match, something she was perfectly capable of doing, provided she paid attention.

Dashed pretty hands. So soft. So touchable. His own words continued to haunt Andrew long after he'd spoken. Nevertheless, there were important facets of their relationship he needed to examine. Or perhaps reexamine would be more accurate. Up to now he'd operated on the assumption that he and Jenny would have to part when he resumed his diplomatic career. But in light of his discovery of her clever brain, it now occurred to him that perhaps his father had been right to insist that she could be taught whatever skills she lacked in order to take her rightful place beside him.

"Checkmate!"

Her triumphant crow proved tantamount to a bucket of ice water dumped over Andrew's head. His dark blue eyes stared dumbfounded at the chessboard and then narrowed to slits as he gazed at his wife in stony disbelief.

Seeing that Andrew was disgruntled, Jenny steeled herself for a wrathful outburst. But instead of the angry outpouring she anticipated, after an exceedingly uncomfortable lull, Andrew's mouth twitched and he burst into gales of laughter. Confused by his unexpected behavior, Jenny decided to wait and see what he did once he regained control of himself.

At last Andrew wiped his eyes with the back of his hand and exclaimed, "Why, you wily little goose. You've gulled me again."

For the first time in what seemed like ages, but were actually only minutes, Jenny felt it safe to indulge in a sly grin.

"Come along with me, sweetheart," he said gruffly as he pulled her to her feet. "I don't think we'll wait for the tea tray after all."

Jenny couldn't help but note the dangerous glint in his eyes. Stalling for time, she protested, "Oh but, Andrew, I was looking forward to a soothing cup. And to tell the truth, you look as if you could do with one as well. Could we not wait until—"

Jenny did not get to complete her sentence, much less raise further objections, because at that point Andrew scooped her up and marched from the study. He was halfway up the flight of stairs before a footman bearing the tea tray appeared in the hall below.

Andrew called down to him, "Bring our tea up to my wife's sitting room. Her ladyship desires a cup before we retire."

"Very good, my lord."

Andrew resumed his rapid pace as he strode down the hall.

"Gracious me, what's your hurry?" Jenny finally worked up the nerve to ask.

Mischief glittered in his dark blue gaze. "Funny you should ask. I, madam, can hardly wait to exact suitable revenge upon you for daring to gull your lord and master twice in one evening."

Perched on a willow branch suspended above the gurgling brook, Jenny left off sketching the peaceful October pastoral scene to hazard a peek at Andrew, who sat with his back slouched against the willow's sturdy trunk. Although he clutched a fishing pole in his right hand, Jenny suspected he'd nodded off. She couldn't tell for sure because the disreputable-looking straw hat he wore had slipped down over his eyes.

A chuckle escaped her. The debonair Corinthian who'd sneered at her best black silk before the wedding ceremony had been transformed into a country bumpkin. Jenny's gaze narrowed. She may have fallen in love with him the instant she'd set eyes on him, but after he'd spoken to her so coldly, she would have cried off if she'd had any feasible alternative.

Now, close to five months later, she was glad she hadn't backed out. True, the entire first month after they'd wed he had been so icily distant she could scarcely bear it. But gradually he'd thawed.

Another thing. Andrew no longer dressed like a walking testimonial to the expertise of his London tailor. Indeed, his relaxation of rigid sartorial standards had so distressed his valet that Parsons had been packed off on an extended holiday. Judging by the venomous look Parsons had tossed her before his departure, Jenny suspected he blamed her for his master's defection.

Another chuckle escaped her. Oh well. Much as she deplored being on the outs with anyone, better the valet than her husband. She was glad Andrew had adopted the habit of dressing for comfort rather than to impress; she no longer felt like a hopeless dowd in comparison.

Jenny smiled. Nowadays, whenever her husband looked at her, she no longer read contempt in his gaze.

The sharp tug upon the fishing line almost jerked the pole from Andrew's relaxed grip. His transition from peaceful slumber was so abrupt, he awoke swearing a blue streak.

Startled by his sudden movement and colorful vocabulary, Jenny lost her balance and tumbled from the tree limb into the brook. Her gasp of surprise proved fortuitous in that her mouth clamped shut before her head went under. Scared witless when she hit bottom, she clawed her way back to the surface, gasping for air. Her arms flailed madly in a desperate effort to stay afloat despite water-laden skirts and half boots that weighed her down. Panic pervaded every cell as she felt the swift current pull her along. She barely had time to draw another deep breath before she again submerged. Her lungs felt ready to burst by the time her head broke the surface for the second time. Her body was tiring; her courage was waning. More to the point, she questioned how much longer she could fight against the inexorable force that seemed determined to drag her under.

As she sank for the third time, she realized that she could actually drown. A plethora of regrets assailed her: regret to be dying so young; regret that they'd never make exquisite love again; regret that she lost all chance of Andrew ever falling in love with her.

Jenny retained only the dimmest memory of being plucked off the brook's bottom and deposited on the mossy bank, only the haziest awareness of Andrew working feverishly to push the water out of her lungs. Indeed, by the time he was satisfied that she'd expelled all she'd swallowed, her ribs ached and she was too exhausted to wiggle a toe.

Just the same, curiosity goaded her to open her eyes. Andrew looked the picture of frustration as he tugged at his sopping wet riding boots. She glanced ruefully at her sodden skirts, then shifted her gaze back to her husband, still engaged in a fruitless tug of war with his recalcitrant boots.

A slightly hysterical giggle escaped her. Andrew glared at her icily. Her numb brain recoiled. Was he angry with his boots or with her? How ugly she must look with her hair hanging in lank strings and her muslin gown clinging to her—no doubt delineating every bulge of her overplump figure.

She finally garnered the courage to raise her gaze to meet his. It was a mistake! The disdain she saw in his dark blue eyes tore her modest cache of hard-won self-confidence to shreds.

"Come, Jenny. I must get you home before you catch a chill."

Andrew barely managed to get her up onto her sidesaddle before he mounted himself. Chagrined by the ungainly figure she cut, her flaming cheeks had barely cooled by the time they reached the hunting box. Indeed, her embarrassment was so painful, she refused to stir from her room for the rest of the day. Nor did she dine with her husband that evening. She ate off a tray she'd ordered sent up, convinced she was doing him a favor by not showing up for dinner. Supping night after night with someone as plain as she must be hard on his digestion.

Andrew was so annoyed when Jenny failed to join him for dinner, he decided to let her sulk. And to underscore his displeasure, for the first time since they'd exchanged vows, he elected not to seek her out and carry her to the bed they'd shared since they'd married.

Jenny was so hurt when she realized Andrew had no intention of coming to her room to insist she share his bed, she cried herself to sleep. By the next morning, however, her courage came surging back. Cotton pads soaked in witch hazel helped alleviate the worst of the puffiness about her eyes, and once dressed, she left her room determined to put yesterday's humiliation behind her.

But despite the best of intentions, Jenny's plans came to naught because shortly after she walked into the morning room, she keeled over in a dead faint. She awoke on the drawing-room sofa. When she struggled to sit, Andrew pushed her gently but firmly back down.

"No, don't attempt to arise yet."

"Whyever not?"

"You fainted."

"I did? How very odd."

"I've summoned a doctor," he said quietly.

"Because I swooned?"

"Yes."

"But I'm not ill, just a bit . . . giddy."

"No doubt today's fainting spell is merely the aftermath of yesterday's misadventure, but it won't hurt to be certain, will it?"

Searching his face, the genuine concern she detected helped mitigate her irritation at having to submit to an examination by a strange doctor.

"I suppose not."

Once her dizzy spell subsided, Jenny managed to retire to her bedchamber with the aid of her husband's sturdy arm to lean upon. Thus, when Dr. Ellers showed up an hour later, Andrew was waiting to take him up and introduce him to Jenny.

The physician possessed a shock of silver hair, and his age instantly won a nervous Jenny's confidence. His bedside manner soon won her trust.

A chambermaid arrived with the hot water Dr. Ellers requested. Dismissing her, Ellers shed his morning coat and rolled up his sleeves. Noting Andrew's raised eyebrow, he gave a good-natured chuckle.

"My mentor at the school of medicine holds with the notion that washing one's hands thoroughly before examining each patient cuts down on the danger of infection."

"Quite," said Andrew.

Her husband's dubious expression amused Jenny. Obviously he wasn't quite convinced that he hadn't summoned a lunatic to attend her. Serves him right for making a mountain out of a molehill, she silently grumbled.

Dr. Ellers patted his hands dry with the fluffy towel provided, then caught Andrew's eye. "Lord Temple, I believe your wife will feel more at ease if you withdraw."

Andrew bristled. "Withdraw?"

The doctor nodded gravely. "No offense intended, my lord. Your wife is shy. I believe she'll feel more at ease without an audience."

"Very well." Andrew bowed stiffly.

His departure left Jenny feeling utterly deserted. Panic rose in her throat. Happily Dr. Ellers proved sensitive to her distress and set to work calming her fears. Initially the questions he asked as he listened to her pulse and peered inside her ears and throat were deliberately innocuous, designed more to set her mind at ease than to extract vital information. Thus, when he finally explained the need to examine her more fully, he encountered only token resistance.

Once finished, he strode over to the commode to rewash and dry his hands. Jenny could only be grateful his back was turned as she struggled to contain her latest wave of embarrassment. By the time he faced her again, her cheeks were no longer so rosy, but unhappily for her, Dr. Ellers launched a fresh round of probing questions.

"Does my lady recall the approximate date her last menses flowed?" he inquired gently.

Flustered, Jenny didn't know where to look.

"No need to be shy. Monthly menses are a natural occurrence in women able to bear children."

His comment set her counting. She could almost feel her eyes growing rounder once she'd arrived at a total.

The doctor smiled benignly. "Understanding dawns. How long has it been?"

"Since I married."

"Your husband mentioned you're on a honeymoon. When were you married?"

"Early in May."

"Four and a half months ago?"

Jenny nodded.

"I see. Tell me, have you suffered any bouts of morning sickness?"

"No, sir."

"Excellent, excellent!"

"Do you mean to say I'm increasing?"

"Of a certainty! I wager in another four or five months you'll be a mother."

Jenny had just begun to wonder if his benevolent smile was a permanent fixture when it faded.

"You appear to be in excellent health, my lady. Even so, no horseback riding. In its place, I prescribe regular carriage airings and short walks. Do nothing strenuous and get plenty of rest." He closed his black doctor's case with a snap. "Any questions before I go?"

"None, sir."

"If you think of any later on, or should you feel unwell, don't hesitate to summon me. Shall I inform your husband of the happy event on my way out?"

Jenny thought for a moment, then shook her head. "I prefer to tell him myself."

"As you wish, ma'am."

An instant after the doctor's departure, Jenny had second thoughts. Had she made the right decision? Would it be so wrong to postpone telling Andrew until yesterday's rift had healed? Last night he hadn't come to her. She'd missed him terribly. Once he knew she was increasing, would he cease making love to her? Their shared intimate moments were precious to her. How could she bear their loss? Of course, it wasn't fair to keep Andrew in the dark. Still, she had to admit she was tempted.

A light tap on the door that connected the master suite to hers signaled Andrew's intention to enter. It threw Jenny into a panic since she hadn't yet resolved her inner conflict. But one look at the silly grin on her husband's face convinced her it didn't matter.

"He told you, didn't he?"

"That I'm to be a father? Yes, he did."

"I wanted to tell you. He said I could. He broke his word."

"It scarcely matters, does it?"

"I suppose not," she responded, determined to put a good face on the disaster that had befallen her.

Yet nothing could be more terrible than to love someone who didn't return one's regard. And even though she loved Andrew deeply, impending motherhood came as something of a shock. Jenny's heart ached for what might have been if she hadn't conceived so soon. She'd hoped for more time to strengthen the tenuous bonds between them. Of course the odds were slim that Andrew would ever come to love her. But what threatened to tear her apart was the knowledge that any chance of a permanent relationship had slipped away.

Jenny resolutely blinked away unspilt tears. All too soon her plump figure would burgeon. With her luck, she was almost certain she'd come to resemble a whale. Naturally he'd no longer insist they share the same bed. After all, what man in his right mind would wish to snuggle up to such an ungainly creature?

Andrew would continue to be kind to her, of course. She knew he would—just as she knew he'd cosset her and see to her every comfort right up to the day their child was born. It was afterward that terrified her. That's when he would disappear from her life as soon as could be decently managed.

Four

1811 . . .

Jenny cuddled the soft warm bundle in her arms. A surge of pure contentment enveloped her. Her two-month-old son, Alexander, nestled against her breast. Wrinkling her nose, she relished Sandor's baby smell, consisting of equal parts talcum powder and warm milk.

She gazed at her son with love in her eyes. His tummy now full, he'd fallen asleep. His downy cheek against her sensitized skin felt so good. Just the same, she ought to ring for the nursemaid to whisk him off to his crib. But this was their special time together, and she wanted to share their mutual serenity a bit longer.

The connecting door to the master suite stood slightly ajar. Consequently, although she couldn't hear what was being said in the adjoining room, she did recognize Andrew's voice. No doubt he was conversing with Parsons, who'd recently returned from his long holiday. She gently laid her son down beside her, freeing her hands so she could rebutton the front of her nightrail. A mischievous grin animated her features. Andrew's valet still didn't know what to make of his master's wife. Oh well, at least his manner toward her was less starchy.

As Jenny recradled her sleeping son, her attention was caught by the soft May breeze that wafted from the open window, causing muslin curtains to billow. It was a balmy day—far too pleasant to entertain gloomy thoughts. But with the time fast approaching when Andrew would leave, it was hard to be cheerful.

To be frank, she didn't understand why he was still here. The terms of the original bargain had been met. There was nothing to keep him in Leicestershire any longer. Her expression grew bleak. Not knowing from one minute to the next when he intended to abandon her strained her nerves to the limit. Yet she couldn't bring herself to ask him what his plans were. He might think she was eager for him to go, and nothing could be further from the truth. Indeed, in her secret heart of hearts, she wished he'd stay with her forever, wished that, somehow or other, theirs could become a genuine marriage. But this was no fairytale. A happy ending was most unlikely. Jenny released a heavy sigh. Much as she hated living in limbo, she dreaded the day that Andrew walked out of her life even more.

"Good morning, sweetheart."

Jenny gave a small, barely perceptible jump, then refocused her gaze. Tall and virile, Andrew

stood framed in the open doorway. He was smiling. A good omen.

"Rise and shine, my dear. I've a surprise for
you."

"You do? What is it?"

"Not so fast. You must eat all your porridge
first."

Jenny gave an unladylike snort. "That's no
hardship. I'm famished."

Andrew chuckled. "No doubt you are, thanks
to our greedy son's demands."

He stared at her so intently, she blushed. With
strong, fluid strides, he closed the distance between them and gently lifted her chin with his
index finger. Jenny met his gaze, but the mischievous gleam in his dark blue eyes troubled her.
Her countenance grew stormy. Was he making
sport of her need to eat for her son's sake?

"My wretched tongue. I shouldn't tease you.
Forgive me?"

His apology had a sincere ring. Or was that
only wishful thinking? Jenny gazed at him searchingly. Unless her eyes deceived her, the mischief
in his had given way to rueful chagrin. Her irritation melted and a delicious warmth stole through-
out her body.

"Forgive you? Why, of course."

*She'd be willing to forgive him anything if only he
didn't desert her. God help her, she loved him!*

She sobered. She dare not tell him though. No
doubt, if he knew how she felt, he'd panic and
leave even sooner.

Andrew reached for Sandor. "Hand him over. I'll carry him up to the nursery while you change. See you at breakfast, my dear."

With a wistful smile, Jenny watched him stride from the room, his sleeping son carefully cradled in his arms. She loved seeing them together. Enjoyed seeing the fierce love that blazed in Andrew's eyes whenever he gazed at his firstborn. If only some day, some way, he'd come to love her as much as he did their son.

Jenny sighed. Pointless to grasp at straws. She yanked on the bellpull to summon a maid to help her dress.

A half-hour later, she entered the morning room, where she ate a hearty breakfast while Andrew perused the *London Times*. Once sated, she waited impatiently for him to set it aside. Frankly, what he found so interesting in a two-day-old paper puzzled her.

At last, he shoved back his chair and rose. "Come, my dear. There's someone I want you to meet."

Intrigued, she let him lead her up two flights of stairs and into the nursery. As soon as they crossed the threshold, Jenny saw a short, plump woman leaning over her son's crib and crooning a lullaby. Who on earth . . . ? Alarmed, Jenny let go of her husband's arm and darted forward.

"What do you think you're doing? Move away from that crib."

Startled, the woman she addressed rocked back on her heels. Next, she reached with both hands

to straighten a black chip bonnet, dubiously
adorned with a single ostrich feather too limp
and bedraggled to incite the least envy in the
heart of the viewer.

Jenny glared at the usurper. "Who are you?"

Bright, alert eyes, the exact shade of the
woman's royal blue cambric dress, raked Jenny up
and down. "I be Birdie Pamphrey, m'lady. Come
to look after young master."

"Have you, indeed? We'll just see about that!"

Birdie wagged a finger at the viscount. "Shame
on you, Master Andrew. You never said your
wife's dicked in the nob."

He responded with a shout of laughter. "No
such thing, Birdie. I do assure you."

Watching him wipe tears of mirth from his
eyes, Jenny resented the amusement at her expense. She asked in a voice tinged with acid,
"This is your surprise? Birdie Pamphrey?"

He nodded. "Birdie used to be my nurse. I
can't think of anyone else I'd rather have look
after Sandor."

Jenny studied the wary expression in her husband's eyes as he shifted his weight from one foot
to the other, and shortly before the gap in the
conversation grew too marked, he belatedly
added, "With your permission of course."

"Of course," Jenny echoed dryly.

Birdie's eyes lost some of their sparkle as she
said quietly, "I'd a come as soon as wee bonnie
rooster be hatched, ma'am, but me rheumatism
flared up."

Jenny nibbled on her lower lip. She had nothing against the woman and didn't want to hurt her feelings. However, Birdie's health was a factor she couldn't afford to overlook. Why, the woman was well past middle age. What if she couldn't keep up with Sandor once he started to walk?

Andrew cleared his throat. It drew Jenny's attention. "We'll retain the nursemaid. Meg can chase after Sandor while Birdie supervises."

Could her husband actually read her mind? Or was it just a lucky guess on his part? No matter. The arrangement he proposed overrode her reservations.

Jenny awarded Birdie Pamphrey a cool nod. "My husband has such faith in you, I'm sure you'll fill the position admirably."

"Handsomely said, ma'am." Birdie beamed her a warm smile. "I understand you don't depend on a wet nurse."

Jenny thrust out her chin. Shortly after Sandor's birth, Andrew had suggested she hire one, but she wouldn't hear of it. "No. Any objection?"

"Nary a one. 'Tis a grand start in life you be giving Master Alexander."

Birdie's wholehearted approval broke the ice and Jenny's expression softened. Andrew had never really understood why she'd insisted on nursing Sandor, but Birdie did. Perhaps they were kindred spirits. Besides, while Birdie might be older than was ideal, her movements were spry. And Meg would be there to help. Jenny could relax. Her son would be in good hands.

Andrew's good-humored chuckle caused her to look at him inquiringly. Eyes twinkling, he said, "Now that I'm reasonably certain you don't plan to murder each other, I'll leave you two to get better acquainted."

Jenny lifted the cloth from her son's burning forehead and dipped it into a basin of cold water. If only Sandor's fever would break. Tears welled in her eyes. Angrily she wiped them away. This was no time to play the watering pot. Her son needed her nursing skill to pull him through. She wrung out the cloth and spread it across his brow, then replaced the folded back sheet flap. At times like this, motherhood was frightening. Her lower lip trembled. It had all started with Sandor's croup. Now his lungs were congested and his temperature was high.

"How's the makeshift steam tent we rigged working?" Andrew asked from the archway.

Jenny's smile was tremulous. "He still has trouble breathing, but I don't think he has to work quite so hard."

"Excellent." Andrew's eyes rapidly scanned the room. Frowning, he asked, "What's become of Birdie and Meg?"

"I ordered them to get a bite to eat and snatch a few hours rest."

"I see." He studied her face. "You look ready to drop yourself. Come sit and put your feet up."

She shook her head. "I dare not. The crises could come at any time."

"Stubborn wench," he grumbled as he placed an arm round her shoulders and led her over to a rocker. "Sit. I'll tend to Sandor."

Gracious, but she was weary. They all were. Dr. Ellers had promised to find them a nurse, but so far no one had shown up on their doorstep.

As Jenny sank down into the rocker, a ghost of a smile touched the corners of her mouth. Even Parsons had pitched in. Bless his heart, he'd helped Andrew rig up the steam tent that she'd insisted would ease Sandor's breathing.

A spasm of wheezy coughs brought Jenny to her feet. She rushed over to Sandor's crib and picked him up. Placing him on her shoulder, she patted his small back and said, "There, there, son. Cough up all that nasty phlegm that's clogging your chest."

As the day advanced, the weary parents took turns tending their four-month-old son. Like a logjam breaking up, time spent under the makeshift vapor tent loosened his congestion. Just before dusk, his fever broke, and his breathing almost normal, he slipped into a deep sleep.

Even so, she couldn't seem to stop herself from peeping under the tent flap every few minutes to make sure he really was all right.

"Any fever?" asked Andrew.

Jenny removed her hand from her son's forehead. "No, he's fine."

"You're sure?"

Jenny nodded. Tears of gratitude welled. As they spilled over, Andrew handed her a clean handkerchief. She was in the process of dabbing her eyes when he swept her up into his arms.

"Andrew, put me down."

"No. You're dead on your feet."

"But we can't leave Sándor alone."

"I'll have a word with Parsons. He can keep watch until Birdie and Meg relieve him."

Jenny was still arguing when Andrew carried her into her bedroom, but nothing she said made a dent in her mate's armor. By the time he'd laid her down upon cool muslin sheets and removed her shoes, she'd decided to save her breath. Yet she continued to feel guilty about leaving Sandor's side. True, he'd seemed better, but things were not always what they seemed. Thus, once Andrew went to speak to Parsons, she tried to rise but found she lacked the strength to sit upright—much less mount a flight of stairs and reenter the nursery.

Indeed, she was so weary that when Andrew returned from his errand and started to undress her, she was capable of only a half-hearted protest. With deft efficiency he divested her of her clothes, slipped her nightrail over her head, and tucked the bedcovers around her.

"There now, sweetheart, get some sleep. You deserve it."

Andrew was almost through the door when Jenny pleaded softly, "Please don't go. Stay with me."

He returned to her side. She reached out her hand. He took hold of it. "You're trembling. What's the matter?"

"Oh, Andrew, he could have died," said Jenny, then burst into tears.

"Well, he didn't. So dry your eyes, sweetheart, and go to sleep."

Good advice. Only it didn't work. The harder she tried to stem her tears, the harder she sobbed. Finally Andrew pulled off his boots and crawled in beside her. Lying in her husband's comforting embrace felt so good. With a faint smile, Jenny drifted into a sound sleep.

Andrew awoke around midnight. Arising, he went to check on his son and found Birdie rocking him. When she saw Andrew, she stopped. Sandor whimpered in protest.

"I've been trying to stave him off so as not to disturb her ladyship, but he be hungry."

"Hungry? If I don't miss my guess, he's ravenous."

"Be her ladyship awake?"

"No, but she'll be furious if I don't take him to her. Give him to me. I'll bring him back once he's drunk his fill."

Standing beside Jenny's bed with Sandor in his arms, a sense of contentment filled Andrew as he gazed at his sleeping wife. Jenny stirred and, as if too warm, threw off her covers. He eyed the outline of her firm breasts covered only by the sheer muslin of her gown. Quite lovely really. He'd been wrong to try to forbid her to nurse

Sandor. There were few sights more beautiful than a mother nursing her child.

And speaking of beauty, while nothing could change the fact that Jenny was rather plain, if there was such a thing as a soul, hers was beautiful. Indeed, asleep or awake, she possessed a glow that radiated from within.

Andrew shook his head in wonder. The notion that her intelligence could amply compensate for her lack of beauty continued to excite him. Chiefly because compared to Castlereagh's wife Emily, Jenny was a raving beauty. Yet as far as he knew, no one had ever dared suggest to the Foreign Secretary that Emily had a deleterious effect on his rise to the top of his profession. On the contrary, not only was Emily considered an asset by her husband's peers, but Castlereagh, despite being an inordinately handsome man himself, clearly doted on his dowd of a wife.

Andrew's excitement reached fever pitch. Jenny was young and malleable. And although he'd hesitated to put his plan in action while she'd been increasing or afterward while she slowly rebuilt her strength, now seemed the ideal time to make a concerted push to see if he could coax her into acquiring the necessary poise and polish needed to be a credit to him in the diplomatic milieu. If he could accomplish that, they need not ever part.

Sandor rooted about his father's warm chest, then whimpered, causing Andrew to recollect his errand.

"Easy there, lad," he advised, then called softly, "Dearest, wake up. I've brought Sandor."

Her eyelids opened then closed. Sandor wailed. Still half asleep, Jenny began to undo the buttons of her nightrail. With a tender smile, Andrew laid his son in his wife's arms.

Later, after returning his sated offspring to Birdie's care, Andrew retraced his steps to Jenny's room. Her eyes were closed. His gaze softened as he studied her. A delicate flush stained her cheeks. She really did have a wonderful complexion. He touched her soft, pliant skin. It had the fine-grained texture of a newborn babe's.

Jenny rubbed her eyelids with her knuckles and peered up at Andrew. *Hold me, please hold me,* she silently pleaded.

With a gruff sigh of surrender, Andrew shed his clothes and climbed in beside her.

The next time Jenny woke, Andrew was gone and she was starving. She rang for a servant. When the upstairs maid appeared, Jenny asked how Sandor was. Only when reassured he'd suffered no relapse did she order a luncheon tray and a bath. When the maid left to do her biddings, Jenny leaned back against her pillows to wait.

But a glimpse at the bedraggled bedclothes refreshed her memory. Angels defend us! They'd made love till dawn. A surge of red-hot color seared her cheeks.

Her eyes widened as she realized that by making love to her, Andrew had reneged on their bargain. Whatever had gotten into him? She wondered. Had it been only a momentary whim? Jenny flinched at this unpalatable thought, then firmly rejected it. Granted Andrew had a hard, implacable side, but she'd never known him to be deliberately cruel. And while she knew he didn't love her, she did think he'd grown reasonably fond of her.

The question of his motives continued to nag. What did Andrew's unexpected resumption of lovemaking mean, if anything? Hope flared to life. Had he had a change of heart? Could it be that he wished to shuck their original bargain?

Jenny sighed. Only time would tell if it were a true turning point in their relationship. But whatever happened, last night's shared intimacy had been a wondrous experience she would always treasure.

Five

Jenny absent-mindedly chewed on the wooden end of the sable-tipped paintbrush. The oak leaves looked resplendent dressed in their autumn colors, which ran the gamut from vivid orange-reds to more subdued purplish hues, and she wanted to do them justice.

When she'd set up her easel, the sun felt warm on her back and a gentle breeze rustled the scattering of leaves that had not as yet fallen. But gradually the sky became overcast and the wind quickened. Absorbed in capturing the scene before her, Jenny scarcely noticed until a particularly ferocious gust threatened to tip over her easel. Leaping forward, she steadied it, then took a few steps backward.

Suddenly her shoulders were cloaked in a comforting warmth as her unseen benefactor draped a kashmir shawl about her. She caught a whiff of the musk scent her husband favored and smiled. One of his hands squeezed her shoulder. She reached up to cover it with hers.

Dearest Andrew, she thought. Ever eager to cosset her. How she prayed she might tell him how much she adored him. But even if the time were right, she doubted she'd ever muster the courage.

She nibbled on her lower lip, wishing that she and Andrew could drift in this enchanted isolation forevermore. Impossible, of course. As a matter of fact, a sennight ago he'd made her promise to give serious thought to accompanying him to Town for the little Season. But, coward that she was, she kept putting him off. Not that she was stupid. Indeed, she recognized with each passing day she risked alienating him further. Yet she couldn't seem to come to grips with her fears, even though she sensed he was losing patience with her.

Truth be told, she was terrified that if she tried to move in such elevated circles, she'd somehow disgrace him. And equally terrified if she didn't yield, he'd leave without her.

"Pack up your paints, sweetheart. There's a sharp nip in the air. Didn't you notice?"

Turning to face him, her expression was wry. "Not until the wind almost knocked over my easel."

"Too absorbed in your paint box, no doubt." The look he shot her was ripe with tender exasperation. "You deserve a scold. You must take better care of yourself. Şandor depends on you."

She awarded him a winsome smile. "He depends on you as much as he does me."

"Nonsense! As his mother you're essential to him, particularly in his infancy."

A tiny frown puckered Jenny's brow as she repacked the wooden case that held her paints and brushes. Did Andrew actually believe a father's guidance was not equally important until Sandor was older? She sighed. Of course he did.

Jenny's thoughts continued to percolate as they entered the hunting box arm in arm. What a ninny she was to assume otherwise simply because of the way Andrew had pitched in when Sandor had taken ill in June. Clearly her crack-brained notion that her husband's understanding of his parental role was somehow superior to that of his peers was wishful thinking on her part.

Andrew halted at the bottom of the staircase. Although he took pains to appear unruffled on the surface, inwardly his nerves were stretched taut. Little wonder. Jenny's constant vacillation was fast becoming untenable.

"Shall we repair to my study? We need to talk."

"Oh? About what?"

He snorted. "Pray do not insult my intelligence by pretending you don't know what's on my mind. In short, do you, or do you not, intend to accompany me to Town?"

Jenny eyed him speculatively. The game was up. Andrew had her neatly cornered. Not that she could blame him. A frank discussion was long overdue. Nonetheless, she dreaded the confrontation so much she couldn't resist yet another stalling tactic.

"Now is not a propitious time for this discussion. Unless of course you don't mind facing a kitchen rebellion by setting back dinner."

Andrew's lips twitched. "Indeed, I'm not that brave. But we differ on the time factor. A half-hour remains before we must dress for dinner. Ample time to air your decision."

"But I need to stow my painting gear."

"I'll do it for you later. Now then, if you will kindly step into my study."

Bowing to the inevitable, Jenny soon found herself established in an armchair that guarded the hearth while Andrew sprawled in its twin.

"Take pity on me, sweetheart. I cannot bear the suspense any longer. Do you accompany me to Town or are you too hen-hearted?"

"Hen-hearted? No such thing! Any hesitancy on my part stems from my reluctance to join in the frivolous pursuits so popular in *tonnish* circles."

He threw her an incredulous look. "My dear, you are definitely an original. Most wives would snap up an offer to take in a London Season."

"Why not look on the bright side? Think of all the blunt you'll save because I've no taste for preening."

Andrew stared at Jenny deeply. Perhaps the answer lay in her past. He must discover why she was being so contrary, as time was running out on him.

His eyes drifted to a low-burning fire on the grate, then back to Jenny. How ironic that, despite all his diplomatic training, he couldn't seem to manipulate his own wife.

A self-deprecatory grin curved the corners of

his mouth upward. "Perchance were either of your parents a confounded Methodist?"

"Certainly not! Both were died-in-the-wool Anglicans."

Andrew chuckled. "No need to comb my hair. I was merely trying to pinpoint the source of your prejudice."

Jenny glared at him. "Do you mean to imply there's no truth to my assessment of the *ton*?"

"Of course not! Nonetheless, it is most unfair to condemn society as a whole on the basis of a few loose screws. Do you not agree?"

"I don't mean to do that. Society may do whatever it pleases with my blessings. 'Tis merely that I have no interest in joining its ranks."

"A pity that. I'd hoped to persuade you to a more tolerant view."

"You think me unreasonable. How very lowering."

He shrugged. "What other conclusion can I draw? After all, you've never set foot in London, have you?"

Andrew kept such a close eye on her, Jenny felt like a defenseless doe caught in a steel trap.

"Well, have you?" he goaded.

"No, I have not," she admitted.

"Jenny, give London a chance. There's more to it than the social treadmill. There's the theater, the Italian Opera, art exhibits, Astley's Circus—"

"Astley's Circus," Jenny whispered. Visibly paling, she burst into tears.

Her sobs were heartwrenching. Appalled, Andrew jumped to his feet. Jenny seldom ever cried. His hand trembled as he reached out to her. He had no idea whether he'd be able to comfort her or not. But he at least had to try.

His brow furrowed, Andrew scooped Jenny up in his arms and settled himself in her chair. He held her on his lap and rocked her as one would a distraught child.

She cried so hard her tears soaked through his shirt front. Still, he held her cradled in his arms while his magical fingertips gradually eased the knots of tension between her shoulder blades and at the nape of her neck. And when her tears finally lessened to a trickle, he mopped her eyes with a clean handkerchief, then held it to her nose and demanded she blow.

"Feeling better?"

She awarded him a quick, shy nod.

"Sweetheart, I don't mean to pry, but what in God's name set you off?"

His query prompted a watery giggle. Not to be put off, he demanded gruffly, "Tell me."

Jenny gave a painful swallow. In view of her outburst, she supposed she did owe him an explanation. "When you mentioned Astley's, the memory of Papa's broken promise touched me on the raw."

"I had not realized your father was cruel to you."

"Indeed not! A trifle too preoccupied with his scholarly pursuits perhaps. But cruel? Never!"

The chiming of the stately clock in the entrance hall informed Andrew it was time to change for dinner. Yet their present conversation was too important to postpone. He rang for a servant and, when a footman appeared, stated, "Find Merton and inform him I wish dinner set back a half-hour."

Once the door closed behind the servant, Andrew returned his full attention to Jenny. "I am pleased to hear your father did not mistreat you. Nevertheless, something in your past troubles you. Tell me about your childhood. Don't leave anything out."

Jenny heaved a sigh. Recognizing she'd have no peace until she satisfied his curiosity, she launched into her sorry tale with as good a grace as she could muster. Initially she stumbled over her words, but once she got past the first few sentences, the story of her sad childhood came tumbling out.

"Mama was completely frivolous. She cared more for stylish gowns and smart equipage than she did for me and Papa. Regardless of expense, you may be sure she never missed a single London Season."

Andrew swore under his breath. Having firsthand knowledge of how much it hurt to be rejected by one's own mother, his heart went out to Jenny.

"So it's your mother who turned you against society."

Jenny nodded. "I threw a temper tantrum when I was about four years old. Mama was furious because my tears spotted the bodice of her silk travel ensemble. To punish me, she refused to kiss me goodbye. Papa dried my tears and promised to take me to Astley's Circus when I was older.

"Unhappily for me, by the time I was old enough to go, Papa was too far up the River Tick to afford such a treat—thanks to Mama's extravagance. She died when I was seven. By then, Papa had a hard time just keeping a roof over our heads and food on the table."

Ashamed of the pathetic tale, Jenny buried her burning face in her husband's damp shirt. Her complexion had barely returned to normal when he suddenly stood and set her on her feet.

Cut adrift, her next words reflected her sense of rejection. "Perhaps now you understand why I've no desire to be decked out in silks and satins in order to join the daily promenade at Hyde Park."

His own spirits crushed by his failure to persuade Jenny to bow to his wishes, Andrew reluctantly conceded, "Yes, I understand perfectly."

"Then I don't have to go to London if I prefer not to?"

Expression rueful, he shook his head. "No, you don't."

The grandfather clock in the entry hall tolled the hour. And even though Andrew had never felt less like smiling in his life, he managed a reasonable facsimile as he offered his wife his arm.

"Come, my dear, I'll escort you to your room so you can dress for dinner."

Ten minutes later, Andrew slipped back into his study and slammed the door. He felt as if he'd just run a marathon. Worse, the walls of his chest seemed like a vise steadily tightening, making each breath he drew progressively more painful.

To distract himself, he cast an appreciative eye about the room he regarded as his private cubbyhole—at least during daytime hours. Its color scheme was limited to various shades of brown enlivened by bold touches of red. It contained three armchairs upholstered in rich cordovan leather secured by brass studs. Two hugged the hearth while the third perched behind a burnished mahogany desk. Flocked crimson wallpaper covered two walls; leather-bound volumes graced built-in bookshelves that encompassed the remaining two.

Clearly both color scheme and furnishings had been chosen to appeal to masculine taste. And what man didn't crave a snug retreat where he could let down his guard? Andrew came here whenever he felt out of sorts or when he needed to think.

By rights, he mused, he should be up in his dressing room submitting to Parsons's ministrations. However, he desperately needed to get a grip on himself first. The realization that he'd come within a whisker of coercing Jenny to accompany him to London had left him thoroughly shaken.

Yet, much as he disliked the idea of parting, it was quite wrong of him to exert undue pressure in order to change her mind. Unfortunately for his plans, Jenny was not socially ambitious. Nor could she be lured to Town by the promise of fashionable gowns. On the contrary, given a choice, Jenny clearly preferred to reside in the country—even if it meant being separated from her husband.

Ah, there's the rub, Andrew conceded with painful candor. A constant procession of rich, well-born, accomplished beauties had spoiled him. His past liaisons had not prepared him for someone with Jenny's fortitude. In his conceit, he'd naturally assumed Jenny would set aside her fears and reservations merely to please him. No wonder he found her marked preference for the country a particularly bitter pill to swallow.

Yet swallow it he must. Because he certainly wasn't going to beg her to accompany him to Town. No, the matter was settled. Jenny preferred to remain here at the hunting box and here she'd stay.

Andrew gazed at the portrait of his mother. The oil painting immortalizing her beauty hung above the Adam's mantelpiece that topped off the hearth. Andrew had only vague recollections of playing nearby while she'd posed for Sir Joshua Reynolds. Still, he supposed such a shadowy memory was only to be expected since he'd been barely three years old at the time. For some reason, the portrait never failed to catch his eye. Andrew wasn't quite sure why. It couldn't be sentiment. He'd scarcely known the woman. Perhaps it was because it represented the sole intrusion of femininity into an otherwise exclusively masculine bastion.

He wrenched his gaze from the portrait. His mother was long dead. Fruitless to dwell on what might have been had she not gone off to Italy with her lover, leaving her small son behind.

Irritated because he'd allowed his thoughts to be sidetracked, Andrew gave his neckcloth a good yank. Time had run out on him. He must come to a decision, and the choice he had to make was painful. He frowned. This was all the more painful because he'd actually believed he could succeed in bringing his country-bred wife up to snuff.

But instead of the success he'd anticipated, scant minutes ago he'd finally come face to face with failure. Not that he hadn't seen it coming. He had. He just hadn't wanted to admit to himself, much less anyone else, that nothing he did seemed to work.

Andrew sank into one of the armchairs that flanked the hearth. The bleak expression in his eyes deepened as his thoughts continued to revolve around Jenny. All summer, he'd pursued his campaign to encourage her to develop broader interests. Alas, she'd resisted every single one of his overtures.

He'd led off by suggesting that she might peruse the *London Times* in order to keep abreast of current news. And to her credit, she'd developed a lukewarm interest in its contents. However, all the rest of his suggestions had fallen on deaf ears, including the one to engage a dance master to teach her both to dance and to move with more grace. Ditto his offer of a complete new wardrobe of gowns or his offer to hire a professional dresser skilled at showing her mistress off to advantage. Nor had any of his broad hints that she might take in the little Season sparked her interest. He gave a short, bitter laugh. So much for his brilliant diplomatic skills! When disaster loomed on the domestic horizon, evidently he was just as helpless to avert it as the next man. Though God knows, he'd tried.

He glanced at the letter clutched in his hand. It bore the official seal of the British Foreign Office. Andrew had been expecting it for weeks. Actually, if it hadn't come soon, he would have considered dashing up to Town to wangle an interview with Castlereagh. Because knowing that he'd failed to mold Jenny into the type of wife who'd be a credit to him, there was little point in sticking around any longer. Besides, his career had been on hold for eighteen months, and unless he was reassigned to a foreign embassy soon, his future in diplomacy would be sure to suffer.

So why did he hesitate? Why couldn't he bring himself to break the wax seal? Could it be because accepting a foreign post meant leaving wife

and son behind, something he was loath to do?
Which was understandable, he supposed. In the
six months since Sandor's birth, a close bond had
sprung up between himself and his infant son.
No doubt tearing himself away from the babe
would have been easier if he'd left as originally
planned, right after he'd introduced Birdie into
the household. Fool that he was, instead of leaving, he'd kept putting off his departure. Then
Sandor had fallen ill and he'd helped take care
of him. After such a bad scare, Andrew had been
too terrified to leave until assured that his son
enjoyed robust health once more.

By then, it had been midsummer, a time when
Parliament adjourned and everyone deserted
London for the countryside, so there'd been no
point in leaving until autumn.

Unfortunately when he'd made that decision,
he hadn't considered the effect of his prolonged
stay on his relationship with his wife. No question
they'd grown closer during the six months he'd
lingered after their son's birth. As for Jenny herself, despite her mulish refusal to grow and
change, for the most part she'd been such a delight that for days on end he had actually forgot
how plain she was. Even more telling, despite the
fact that he didn't love her, there was no denying
that he'd grown deuced fond of her.

But now it was September. Time for Parliament
to reconvene. Time for the little Season to begin
in London. Above all, time for Andrew to wrench
himself free of domestic encumbrances—else he'd

never go. And if he never went, he knew he'd regret such a maggoty impulse and doubtless take his resentment out on Jenny, who did not deserve such Turkish treatment.

No. Much as it pained him, he must leave before he became so firmly entrenched he'd lose his will to sever the bond that had grown between them.

Andrew crossed to the desk and picked up his letter opener. He slit through the wax seal and read the contents. Just as he'd thought, the letter summoned him to Town and hinted that a diplomatic post was in the offing.

Should he vacillate, Andrew knew the Foreign Secretary would not hesitate to wash his hands of him. Make no mistake. He must seize the moment.

Six

Gazing into the looking glass above her dressing table, Jenny watched Dora's nimble fingers school her fluffy hair into some semblance of order.

"There now. I be done dressing your hair. What jewelry does madam desire to wear?"

"Choose for me, Dora. I'm too busy reveling in my last-minute reprieve to think straight."

The abigail's ruddy cheeks flushed with pleasure as she opened the lid of her mistress's jewelry box and scowled at its contents. After due deliberation, she lifted a topaz necklace.

"How's about this? 'Twill set off your bronze satin to a nicety."

The abigail was right. The necklace would complement her gown. Jenny beamed her a smile. "You've excellent taste, Dora. Perhaps I should rely on you more often."

She continued to smile. For certain, the choice would please Andrew, who'd presented her with the topaz necklace and matching teardrop earrings on her nineteenth birthday the previous month. Her expression softened. Slowly but surely she was coming to terms with the fact that her husband was an incurable romantic, who'd no doubt still be lavishing her with expensive bits of jewelry when they were both old and gray. Indeed, she was no longer certain she wished to curb his extravagant gestures. After all, it was rather sweet of him to wish to deck his homely wife out in the finest jewels in the kingdom.

"There now, m'lady," Dora announced, once she'd securely anchored both earrings. "You look as fine as sixpence, if I say so myself."

"Thank you. Now scoot along to the kitchen before you miss your supper."

Once Dora had gone, Jenny rose and picked up her fan. All during the time her abigail had fussed over her, Jenny had grappled with a premonition that something was wrong, and even after she'd dismissed the maid, the conviction that all was not well continued to nag. She frowned. If she could just put her finger on what was amiss, she knew she'd feel better. But she couldn't. It was maddening.

Jenny was about to exit her room and join her husband in his study for her customary glass of before-dinner sherry when she heard a resounding thud. She arched an eyebrow. It sounded as if someone had dropped a heavy object. But what on earth could it be?

The thud was followed by a cacophony of raised male voices emanating from the landing. Curiosity primed, she cracked her bedchamber door. It didn't take her long to surmise that the footmen had been carrying a heavy trunk and were presently arguing about whose fault it was that they'd dropped it.

Trunk? More curious than ever, Jenny stepped into the hallway and proceeded on tiptoe. Not a single servant noticed her approach as they were engrossed in their task. Her eyes widened as she stared at the trunk. Terror gripped her as her mind grasped its significance.

Jenny trembled as one after another her thoughts struck with lethal precision. Andrew wasn't wasting a minute leaving her! She'd made it patently clear that the little Season was not to her liking, and he'd chosen London over her. Had that been on his mind all the time they talked? Had he questioned her so closely hoping to demonstrate how unfit she was to join him in social circles?

She felt her heart shrivel in her breast. Her worst nightmare—fears she'd shoved deep into a cobwebbed corner of her mind—bobbed to the surface. God save her! How would she manage without him?

But wait. Perhaps she was jumping to the wrong conclusion. Yes, of course she was. Her fear of desertion was groundless. Her foolish worries were all for naught. Still, she was forced to admit he'd grown quite restless of late. Jenny bit her lip. Stop it! she ordered herself, frantically searching her mind for a more palatable reason for the trunk on the landing.

Light dawned. Why, of course. If she hadn't

let fear get the best of her, she'd have hit on the truth earlier. Andrew had grown tired of trying to reason with someone as bullheaded as she and had decided to override her objections. For her own good, of course. Consequently they were all going on a trip. He hadn't told her yet because he wanted to give her time to recover from her emotional outburst before he laid down the law. More than likely, his intention was to tell her after dinner. Jenny's eyes sparkled. A few weeks in London would be a sure cure for Andrew's recent discontent.

A faint frown disturbed her ivory brow. Good heavens! It would take her ages to pack. Bubbling over with excitement, Jenny entered her husband's bedchamber without bothering to knock. To her disappointment, it stood empty. Deflated, she was about to leave when she heard voices coming from the adjoining room. With a cry of relief, she barged into her husband's dressing room.

"Andrew, you rogue. You might have warned me that the three of us are taking a trip."

Startled, Andrew crushed the neckcloth he'd been arranging to his satisfaction, then stifled a groan as the excitement in his wife's voice registered. God forgive him! Parting was going to be much harder than he'd envisioned. With sinking heart, he discarded the ruined neckcloth and turned to face Jenny.

"Trip? What are you talking about?"

Jenny lightly tapped the back of his hand with

her fan. "You can't fool me. The footmen dropped your trunk in the hall and Parsons is busy packing your valise, is he not?"

Andrew felt acute discomfort. "Yes, well, I was going to tell you after dinner."

"Really, Andrew, it's too bad of you not to tell me straightaway. Have you any idea how long it will take the maids to pack Sandor's things? Silly question. Of course you do not. Pray excuse me, sir. I must set them to work at once."

"For God's sake, Jenny, stop your babbling and listen to me!"

Jenny froze dead in her tracks, then spun round. She looked so dazed, so bewildered, Andrew wanted to spread open his arms and offer her comfort. Instead, he hardened his heart and turned to his valet. "Parsons, I desire a word with my wife. Leave off packing and go settle that fracas in the hall. I'll ring when I need you."

Andrew waited until Parsons had left the room before training his gaze upon his wife. Her normally glowing skin was unnaturally pale, and her eyes held a guarded wariness.

"You don't wish us to accompany you, do you?"

Andrew ruthlessly suppressed an annoying niggle of guilt. "No, I do not. You see, my dear, you were so adamant about your antipathy toward society that you convinced me that any attempt to try to mold you into a more worldly creature would be doing you a grave injustice."

"So your solution to the problem is to desert me?"

"Untrue. That makes me sound callous. I want what is best for both of us."

"And you don't think it callous to go blithely off without me?"

"Please try to understand. I've no desire to make you miserable by dragging you to London, yet I've been ordered to present myself to the Foreign Secretary."

"So it's your intention to leave me behind?"

"It's what you want, is it not?"

With growing perplexity, Andrew watched her eyes take on a haunted look. He'd given her what she wanted. She ought to be jumping for joy. Women! Would he ever understand them?

Being left behind was most definitely not what she wanted! But how could she tell him that without making an utter fool of herself? Jenny's head spun as she desperately tried to think of a way to convince him she hadn't really meant what she'd said. That she'd let childish fears get the best of her. That she'd never meant to imply that she'd be miserable in London.

She felt so mixed up that the right words refused to come. "You're leaving me?"

Andrew wished he could think of some way to lessen the raw pain in Jenny's eyes. But stalling in the vain hope of finding a kinder way to sever the tie between them would only prolong her agony. The sooner he laid all his cards on the table the better.

"Yes, I am. I've set Parsons to packing because I leave at first light."

"Without a word to me?"

"Certainly not. I'd planned to tell you after dinner." He gave a rueful shrug. "Unfortunately you found me out before I had a chance to break the news gently. Pity that."

Jenny visibly stiffened. "Spare me your pity, sir. To be sure, your sudden departure comes as something of a shock. But I'll come about."

"Of course you will," he hastened to reassure her in a voice that sounded a shade too hearty to his own ears. "I apologize for not spelling out my intentions more clearly. I confess I did not think it necessary. After all, we made a bargain. You knew I'd be leaving one day, did you not?"

"I did think so at first, but . . ." Jenny made a visible effort to choke back tears, "when you chose to ignore the terms, I guess I began to assume otherwise." She swallowed with difficulty, then added in a voice tinged with bitterness, "Silly me!"

Andrew flushed. He felt like an errant school-boy called on the carpet for a well-deserved flogging. Curse Jenny for arousing his guilt by calling him to account. Yet, to be fair, he supposed she did have a genuine grievance.

Glancing her way, he was alarmed to see what little color remained in her face slowly drain as she crumpled into a disconsolate heap in a nearby chair. A sharp shaft of guilt stabbed Andrew between the ribs. Damnation! What a selfish beast he'd been to take advantage of Jenny's compliant nature and assert a husband's conjugal rights. By bending the terms of their bargain instead of adhering to them strictly, he'd misled her.

"You're entirely too pale. Can I get you anything?"

"No, nothing. But wait. There is something you can do for me, if only you would."

With difficulty, Andrew managed to cast his features in a jovial mode. "I am at your service. What is it that you desire?"

"Take us with you?"

"Jenny, our son is too small to travel about the globe from pillar to post. As for you, my dear, a moment's thought should suffice to expose the folly of such a course. Only think how uncomfortable you'd feel if thrown into the sophisticated world of diplomacy."

Jenny had the grace to look chagrined. "Very well, I won't tease you on that score. But at least let us come as far as London with you."

"Certainly not. You'd have no idea how to go on and, I might add, absolutely no inclination to learn. No, it's out of the question."

"It's true I've no Town polish, but surely I could learn. Especially with someone with your address to guide me. Do say we may accompany you."

"My dear, if you recall, I tried to lure you to Town by promising to show you the sights. And what was your response? You cried buckets. No, sweetheart. I'm sorry to disoblige you, but no. You may not come."

"Is it because you think Sandor too young to travel?"

"Partly, yes."

"Very well, I'm willing to compromise. We'll leave him here with Birdie and Meg. But please take me with you, Andrew. If only for a few days."

"My dear, I could never be so cruel. A half-hour past, you took great pains to convince me that you're a simple country girl. And you were right to do so. Here you thrive. There you'd flounder like a beached cod."

Jenny winced. "You have the gall to compare me with a fish? How dare you!" A wild laugh tottering on the border of hysteria escaped her. "I knew from the start that ours was not a love match. Yet, fool that I am, I never once imagined that you held me in such low esteem."

"Jenny, do calm down. My analogy was not meant as an insult."

"It scarcely matters. Go then. But never come back. You've worn out your welcome."

"My dear, I never intended to hurt you. As for returning, you needn't worry. Rest assured I shall erase that option from my agenda."

Jenny flinched as if he'd struck her. "Will you, indeed! I find that passing strange. Granted you do not love me, but you do love Sandor. How can you bear to never set eyes on him again?"

"Is that what you think I intend to do? If so, you're mistaken."

"Am I? Perhaps you'd care to enlighten me."

"Certainly. While I expect to see little of Sandor until he's out of leading strings, once he's old enough to go away to school, he will spend part of his holidays with me."

Jenny lifted an eyebrow and said in a voice laced with scorn, "You expect a schoolboy to journey to foreign shores? Gracious! You're even more selfish than I thought."

Andrew struggled to contain his temper. "Jenny, don't misunderstand me. I'm deuced fond of the lad. But while it's within my rights to do so, I don't plan to tear him from your breast. For the next few years, I'm content to leave him in your sole care. And when he's older, I promise you your fair share of his leisure time."

"I suppose I must thank you for not depriving me of my son's company entirely."

"Jenny, I would prefer to part friends. But much as I've enjoyed our country idyll, I long for the stimulus that abounds in worldly circles. I sincerely apologize for any actions on my part that may have misled you as to my intentions. But, friends or no, I leave at first light."

"I quite see that your decision is firm. Godspeed, my lord."

Andrew shot her a guarded look. He could see she was close to tears and silently prayed that she possessed enough pride to spare them both an embarrassing scene. The sound of the dinner gong brought him up short.

He pinned a smile on his face and offered his arm. "Thank you, my dear. But perhaps you should save your good wishes until after dinner."

Jenny shook her head. "I fear one farewell is all I'm up to. As for dinner, I trust you will excuse me. I seem to have lost my appetite."

After a solitary meal made less palatable by dark looks dished up not only from Robert, the footman, but also by Merton, the butler, Andrew was quite ready to retire to his private study for a fortifying snifter of brandy.

What a pity that he'd been forced to be cruel in order to be kind, he mused. Admittedly, his severing the matrimonial bonds had caused Jenny pain, more pain than he'd intended. However, she was very young. She'd get over it.

True, Jenny amused him here in the country, but unfortunately she had neither beauty nor grace to recommend her. And while she had the intellect, she chose to let it lie dormant. It was all very well for her to plead that she could learn, but while he'd be the first to admit she was bright, he was convinced any attempt to groom her for such an exalted position would only lead to failure. And the end result would be that Jenny would be even more miserable knowing she'd been given a chance and had failed. No, best leave her here. True, at the moment she was very unhappy, but he was doing the right thing. She'd made it clear that she had no taste for the role of a diplomat's wife, yet he thrived in that milieu.

Drat his sire's stubborn streak. But for his father's insistence, Andrew would never have married her. Still, marriage to Jenny had had its moments. Besides, if they hadn't married, he wouldn't have a son like Sandor.

Eighteen months was quite long enough to rusticate, he told himself as he tossed and turned in his bed, sleep eluding him. He wished he'd handled things better. He'd been a fool to linger after Sandor's birth. Had he left sooner, he would never have succumbed to the temptation to tamper with their original bargain. Nor would Jenny have been so hurt, since she wouldn't have had a chance to become so attached to him. Yes, it had been a mistake to linger, but there was no way he could alter the past, so it was best not to dwell on it.

Rising as planned after a sleepless night, he hurriedly dressed. He considered taking another peek at his son before he left but feared the boy might wake, and then who knew how long it would be before he could tear himself away.

He chose to ride his own mount during the first leg of his journey. Shifting his horse's gait to a canter to allow the temperamental beast to work off his fidgets, Andrew wished to heaven he could forget the stunned shock he'd seen in Jenny's eyes the exact moment she'd realized he intended to leave her behind.

Devil a bit! His life was about to take a fresh spin. Andrew was eager to embrace the exciting world of diplomacy, eager to return to a milieu that offered both challenge and sophisticated amusements not found in the wilds of Leicester.

Even so, whether he rode alongside his carriage or sat inside while his coachman drove, Jenny's sad face continued to plague him. Indeed, it wasn't until he approached the outskirts of London that its forlorn expression began to fade.

Seven

1812 . . .

Birdsong drifted through the morning room's
open window. A soft May breeze played tag with
sheer muslin panels thrust aside both to offer
ventilation and an unobstructed view of daffodils,
tulips, and patches of violets scattered beneath a
stand of white birch. However, Jenny was too dis-
heartened by the task she'd set for herself to pay
any attention to the charming outdoor scene.

She sat at the small writing desk she used
whenever she went over her household accounts.
Today, however, she wasn't bent over a ledger. She
bit the tip of her tongue, something she uncon-
sciously did whenever she needed to concentrate.
Today, she was writing to Andrew and wanted her
penmanship to be perfect.

Not that he deserved the courtesy, but Jenny
hoped she knew her duty. Andrew had sent only
one letter, written shortly before he'd set sail for
St. Petersburg. By this time, she'd handled it so
much it was about to fall apart. Not that it mat-
tered, as she could recite it word for word.

The expression in Jenny's eyes grew bleak as she called up the letter—each word a coffin nail driven straight into her heart.

> *11 October 1811*
>
> *My dear Jenny,*
>
> *I've been appointed secretary at legation to the British Embassy in Russia. Since I will be out of the country and not easily accessible, I've arranged for your household allowance be deposited in your account at the Melton bank each quarter day. Should you require additional funds, contact my man of business, Silas Minton, at 22 Chancery Lane, London. Minton has discretionary powers to either grant you additional funds to cover unforeseen emergencies or, if deemed necessary, increase your allowance.*
>
> *I am, madam, your most obedient servant,*
> *Andrew Halpern, Viscount Temple*

Although it was a warm day, Jenny couldn't help but shiver. Little wonder. Indeed, if she'd ever, even for a second, imagined that Andrew might one day experience a miraculous change of heart, the letter's icy tone insured that such a foolishly romantic wish would perish from frostbite.

Rubbing her arms vigorously to rid them of goose bumps, she recalled how wretched she'd been the previous autumn, even before his letter came. His abrupt departure in early September had been a terrible blow. Why, even now eight months later, she squirmed with shame whenever she recalled how she'd begged him to take her with him. His incredulous look still made her cringe.

How lowering to be told by the husband she adored that he had no faith in her ability to assimilate the social graces. Of course Jenny knew she was no beauty, but she'd felt this drawback would be overlooked once she acquired the skills to be a good hostess. But Andrew had refused to even let her try. And then while she was still reeling from his desertion, she'd discovered she was again increasing. How dreadful to face her second confinement without Andrew's support. Her first thought was to dash off a note to him before he left London informing him of her condition, but in the end she'd decided not to.

For Jenny was through groveling. Indeed, her former timidity enraged her. And Andrew's callous desertion had so infuriated her that she'd yanked all the stylish gowns he'd given her from her clothespress and tossed them one by one onto the fire.

The melodious peal of the tall pendulum clock that dominated the front hall yanked Jenny from reverie. Burning all those lovely gowns had no doubt been foolish. Still, she had no regrets. She gave herself a small shake. Enough woolgathering. Her letter must go in the next post. But first things first. She must review what she'd written.

5 May 1812

Dear Andrew,
   I am delighted to inform you that you are the

*father of twin sons, christened Alistair William
and Aubrey Curtis Halpern, born 17 April 1812.
Sandor walks—or should I say runs? Birdie chases
after him crying "Slow down, you little rascal,
slow down."*

Affectionately, Jenny

Jenny groaned. Would she never learn? The
last thing Andrew deserved was an affectionate
missive from the wife he shamefully neglected.
With an anguished cry, she ruthlessly crushed the
sheet of vellum. As if protesting such Turkish
treatment, the paper crackled, but Jenny was too
overset to heed it. Furious with herself for letting
down her guard, Jenny rolled the offensive letter
into a ball and tossed it on the floor.

Temples pounding, she held her aching head
in her hands. For goodness sake, stop wearing
your heart on your sleeve! she silently admonished. Stop being a toadeater. Show some backbone.

Once she'd vented her spleen, Jenny took out
a fresh sheet of vellum, dipped her quilled pen
into the inkwell, and once again began to write.

An hour later, the tall pendulum clock chimed.
Jenny thrust the quill pen into the standish and
looked about herself. The pile of crushed paper
balls that ringed her chair triggered an attack of
self-loathing.

Jenny sighed. What on earth was the matter

with her? Why couldn't she dash off a short note to her errant spouse and be done with it?

Rising, she began to pace. Part of the problem, she finally decided, was that she so seldom wrote letters that she'd never developed the knack. After all, who would she write to? She had no girlhood friends—thanks to a scholarly father so intent upon guarding his own privacy that he'd never noticed his daughter lacked playmates.

And since she'd come to live in Leicestershire, her correspondence was limited to penning brief notes to decline invitations. No wonder she felt lonely. She was in dire need of a friend she could confide in and whose advice she could trust.

Jenny was not stupid. She knew the best way to make friends was to make a push to become acquainted with her neighbors. But up until quite recently, she couldn't spare the time. Only consider, she mused. Her honeymoon had segued into pregnancy, followed by Sandor's birth and his near-fatal bout with croup. Then when Andrew had stayed on through the summer months, she hadn't wanted to share him with anyone.

Granted, she was partially to blame for the fact that she had no one to confide in. Even after he'd left her, she'd continued to decline all invitations addressed to Viscountess Temple, mostly because she suspected her neighbors had invited her so that they might pose barbed questions in regard to her husband's defection, and Jenny had known her pain was still too raw to bear their inquisition with equanimity. Once she'd learned she was again with child, to have flaunted her unwieldy self in public would have been certain to scandalize the entire neighborhood. Now, of course, the twins were thriving and she was free to accept any invitation she chose, but, ironically, her neighbors had crossed her off their lists.

A forlorn expression flickered in her eyes. Had Andrew desired it, she'd have been happy to accompany him to neighborhood functions. However, he'd made it plain early in the marriage that he had not the smallest wish to rub shoulders with the local rustics. Jenny's lips achieved a cynical twist. His excuse had been that he'd wanted her all to himself. At the time, she'd been flattered. Naive ninnyhammer that she'd been, she'd swallowed his lie whole. Now, with the advantage of hindsight, she realized that the reason he'd urged her to refuse all invitations was that he didn't want to be seen in public with such an antidote. In short, he'd been ashamed of her.

Jenny winced. At times, his contempt still stung. Less and less often though, thank goodness. Because might-have-beens were futile. One could not change what had already occurred; one could only learn from it. Her newfound sanguinity triggered a wry chuckle.

Reviewing the past was all very well, Jenny conceded, but she still had a letter to write. Admittedly, she faced a task she'd prefer to shirk, yet she felt honorbound to inform her husband of the twins' birth. It rankled that she didn't have Andrew's direction and must send the letter to his man of business with a request that he forward it to her husband.

Part of her problem was that she had not the least desire to write Andrew. To be blunt, she'd rather wrestle a cobra. Knowing her conscience would give her no peace until she did, however, she might as well get it over with. The sooner she did, the sooner she could escape outdoors with her sketching pad. Resolved not to falter again, Jenny returned to the desk, dipped the nib of her pen into the ink bottle, and wrote:

Dear Lord Temple,
  Permit me to inform you that on 17 April 1812, you became the father of twin sons.
  I am, sir, your most obedient servant,

Jenny scrawled her signature satisfied that its tone was as cool and distant as Andrew's. She sprinkled it with sand, folded it in thirds, and affixed a wax seal. Then, taking a blank sheet, she penned a brief note to Silas Minton in London requesting that he forward the enclosed missive to her husband in either Moscow or St. Petersburg, whichever city the Russian court currently graced.

When a footman responded to her summons, she handed him the letter and instructed him to post it in time to catch the mail coach. Once he'd gone, Jenny drew a deep exhilarating breath. There now. She'd finally written to Andrew to tell him about the twins. Birdie would have to stop nagging her.

She gazed at the sea of crumpled paper balls surrounding her chair. Gracious, what a mess! She started to set the room to rights, but Birdie entered before she could make any headway.

"Saints preserve us! What have you been up to?"

Jenny swiftly assumed an angelic demeanor. "I've written to Andrew."

"Good for you. I hope your news cuts up his peace. If he wuz here, I'd box his ears, so I would."

Jenny's eyes widened in amazement. When Birdie had first joined the household, she'd worshiped the ground Andrew trod upon. But now, unless Jenny's ears deceived her, she'd switched her allegiance.

Jenny grinned. "Heavens, Birdie, such ferocity. Lucky for Andrew, he's safely out of reach."

"It be no laughing matter, my lady. Imagine his lordship jauntering off to foreign parts and leaving you behind to fend for yourself with not one, but two buns in the oven!"

Jenny nearly choked on her own laughter. "Buns in the oven? Really, Birdie. Such an indelicate phrase."

"It be the God's truth for all that," she insisted, refusing to be cowed.

Birdie's righteous indignation struck Jenny as hilarious. She tried to suppress a giggle, but it was no use. Overcome, she collapsed in a helpless heap upon the chintz-covered sofa. She laughed until her sides ached and tears streamed down her cheeks.

Birdie shot her young mistress a worried glance and yanked on the bellpull. When Merton appeared, she told him to send a maid to tidy the room, then bided her time with ill-disguised impatience until the butler, much on his dignity, retreated.

"You be in such an odd mood, I almost forgot. The dressmaker be here."

"Excellent. Where did you put her?"

"In the sewing room, m'lady."

Jenny rose from the sofa and went to stand before a large cheval glass buttressed by a set of tall windows. Just as well that she'd burned the gowns Andrew commissioned shortly after they'd wed two years ago, she thought. Not only were they out of style, now that she'd finally shed the last of her baby fat, they'd hang on her like formless shrouds.

Studying her reflection, Jenny turned a little to one side and then the other so she could see more of her silk gown, designed to show off the stylishly slender figure she'd miraculously acquired shortly after she'd given birth to the twins. Indeed, she was so pleased with her newfound svelteness, she couldn't resist preening a little.

Her gown was new, one of several she ordered the minute she'd recovered from her most recent confinement, and its deep russet hue infused a bit of color into her cheeks. And a contrasting color was what she desperately needed to relieve the bland combination of ivory skin, white-blond hair, and eyebrows and eyelashes so pale her dressmaker suspected she bleached them. As if she would. For who in their right mind would want invisible eyebrows and eyelashes? Certainly not Jenny. But she was stuck with them anyway, curse her luck!

With a helpless shrug, she turned away from the mirror and said to Birdie, "If anyone wants me, I'll be in the sewing room."

"Now? It be almost time for lunch."

Jenny suppressed a sigh. She dare not admit that she wasn't especially hungry, because it would overset Birdie and she had no wish to do that. So instead, she pinned a smile on her face and said, "So it is. Very well, I shall eat first and then visit the sewing room."

"Very good, ma'am. If you need me, try the nursery."

Jenny took all her meals in the breakfast room, a practice she'd established shortly after Andrew's departure. Since she must dine alone, she preferred its cozy informality to the dining room with its banquet-length table that she found intimidating.

Jenny allowed Merton to seat her. She spread her napkin across her lap and signaled that she was ready to be served. He and Robert sprang into action. Indeed, she reflected, the entire staff had taken to cosseting her. Birdie, however, was by far the worst offender. Smiling, Jenny gave nodded assent to a wedge of pigeon pie and a side dish of steamed asparagus.

The main course was followed by bread pudding embellished with lemon sauce. It was so rich, Jenny couldn't finish her portion. Replete, she giggled. If Birdie found out she hadn't cleaned her plate, she'd be sure to scold.

Jenny sobered. Truth to tell, but for Birdie, she did not know how she would have managed to go on after Andrew left her. Last autumn had been a horrid time for Jenny. Her spirits had sunk so low that she did not care if she lived or died. She couldn't eat; she couldn't sleep. Indeed, the mere thought of food was enough to tie her stomach in knots. She'd lost weight, of course—not that she'd cared. All she'd wanted was to be put out of her misery.

Dear, loyal Birdie had refused to let her wallow in self-pity. The wily nurse had coaxed and cajoled her to eat with relentless persistence. Come to that, she doubted she'd ever forget Birdie's comment the day Jenny told her she was once again increasing.

"Little wonder you be blue-deviled, m'lady. Master Andrew deserves to be flogged. Still you must eat. If not for your own sake, think of the babe you carry."

After that, Jenny had made a concerted effort to take better care of her health. To be sure, it hadn't been easy, but she must have managed to consume enough food of a sufficient variety, since both twins were healthy.

She pushed back her chair and rose. As she made her way to the sewing room, she continued to ruminate. But for Birdie, she might never have emerged from the depression she'd fallen into when Andrew rejected her. She owed her sons' nurse a debt she could never repay.

Jenny smiled faintly as she approached the sewing room. God knew how she would have managed to cope without Birdie's constantly goading her to drink her milk and eat all her vegetables.

Eight

Entangled in the throes of delirium, Jenny tossed her head from side to side. Birdie hovered nearby, alternately wringing her hands and applying a cold compress to her mistress's fevered brow.

Still writhing, Jenny was only marginally aware of the wet flannel square applied to her burning forehead. Her focus remained firmly fixed upon Andrew, who, while only a few tantalizing steps away, kept eluding her.

Jenny's features took on a mulish cast. No matter. Let him run. This time she was determined to catch up with him. This time he wouldn't escape. This time, she'd follow him to the ends of the earth, if necessary.

"Andrew?" Jenny whispered hoarsely.

His wide-open arms beckoned. Eagerly she rushed forward. But just before she drew close enough to reach out and touch him, his image faded.

"Andrew, wait," she rasped.

A sharp sliver of pain pierced her heart's core.

How very distressing. In the blink of an eye, Andrew was gone.

"Try not to thrash about so, m'lady. It do wear a body out just to watch."

Jenny opened her eyes in time to catch Birdie's worried look. She closed them again, confused. Dear me. What was Birdie doing here? Why wasn't she in the nursery where she belonged? She longed to ask, but her throat was so sore, it hurt to speak. Despite the pain, she needed to ask some questions.

But before Jenny could manage so much as a croak, Birdie forestalled her. "No need to fret. The three babes be fit as fiddles. But you need looking after. You be feverish."

Jenny's brow cleared. She was ill. No wonder she felt weak as a kitten. No wonder her head ached. "My throat hurts."

"So I would imagine. You be thirsty, I make no doubt. Here, let me help you sit up."

Not only did the cool water soothe Jenny's raw throat, it tasted like nectar. However, once Birdie laid her back down, she realized she was still thirsty. How frustrating, she thought. It hurt so much to swallow, all she'd been able to take were a few paltry sips. Her fingertips grazed the hollow at the base of her sore throat. Not only did it ache, a mysterious obstruction seemed intent upon closing off her windpipe.

Once the viscountess fell back to sleep, Birdie burrowed deeper into the generous cushions of a bedside chair, weary to the bone. And no wonder.

A scant fortnight ago, Lady Temple had fallen gravely ill and the doctor, who'd attended her during both confinements, had been summoned. Once Dr. Ellers had examined his delirious patient's throat, he'd told Birdie her mistress had diphtheria and warned that she and anyone else who'd visited the sickbed must be kept isolated from the rest of the household. Furthermore, since it would be most unwise to expose Lady Temple's three infant sons to the highly contagious malady, he'd barred Birdie from the nursery.

The separation from her three charges had almost broken Birdie's heart. However, it would never do to endanger little Alexander's health— nor his baby brothers' either.

A cold draft on her neck prompted Birdie to wrap her shawl more tightly. Although she had a high regard for Meg's competence and had hired two maids to assist her, she couldn't help but worry how her three darling babes fared in her absence.

Birdie gently massaged bone spurs which caused each finger joint to throb painfully. Her nine and forty years sat heavily upon her rounded shoulders, and to be frank, after a fortnight spent tending her sick mistress, she felt considerably older. Ancient really. And to add to her misery, her arthritis had decided to flare up. Of course, plunging her hands into cold water so often—not to mention wringing out the wet cloth—only aggravated the pain in her swollen joints.

A pronounced frown dug deeper ruts into her

normally placid brow. Whatever could Master Andrew have been thinking when he'd gone haring off to Russia of all places? For that matter, what maggot had invaded his brainbox causing him to leave his wife behind at his father's hunting box—especially when her ladyship was breeding?

However, to give the devil his due, it was possible that he hadn't known when he left. Still, the very least he could have done was to answer her ladyship's letter informing him of the twins' birth. It was only common courtesy. Yet, three months later, the viscountess still had not heard from him.

Birdie pressed her lips into a thin line. Her heart went out to the sweet little viscountess. Come to that, it didn't surprise her at all that her mistress had succumbed to diphtheria. Jenny had gone into a decline after Master Andrew's departure. Bearing twins seven months later had further sapped her strength.

Then, near the end of June, the viscountess had sickened. And here it was mid-July already and, what with her poor mistress hovering at death's door, Birdie had to wonder if Jenny would live long enough to celebrate her twentieth birthday in August. Wringing her hands, Birdie scarcely knew where to turn.

The next time Jenny woke, it was to a cacophony of discordant voices engaged in a brangle. Her head rang; her eardrums threatened to burst. In self-defense, she clapped her hands over her ears. While her action did not block off the din completely, it did reduce the distressing dissonance to a tolerable level.

One voice was recognizable; the other was not. But since neither was Andrew's, what did it matter?

"See here, Birdie. I did not hie here from Sticklepath as fast as I could travel to be kept in the dark. How is Jenny?"

"Sick as a cat. But, Lord Buxton, you ought not to have set foot in here."

"Hang the proprieties!" the voice boomed. "She looks terrible. I refuse to stir so much as an inch until you tell me what ails her."

"M'lord, I be glad to open me budget. But not in m'lady's bedchamber. And do lower your voice. Her ladyship needs her rest."

It was several more days before Jenny woke to birdsong wafting through the open window. Lucid for once, she was entirely alone. Eagerly she took advantage of the unexpected respite from constant supervision to sort through her thoughts.

First of all, she'd been ill. Dangerously so. Thus, while grateful that she was finally able to think straight, Jenny quailed as she recalled instances when her mind had been a hopeless muddle. Indeed, there'd been times when she'd felt she was in a living nightmare. More frightening were the times she'd seemingly conjured up her errant husband out of thin air. An obvious hallucination, she conceded.

Snatches of random memories almost too pain-

ful to recall intruded. Jenny winced. At times
she'd ranted and raved as if demented. How
dreadful to lose control of herself like that. But
worst of all, she had no idea how she'd acted
during those times when she'd been too delirious
to remember anything at all.

Like a relentless tide, weariness enveloped her.
Her eyelids drooped. Silence broken only by birdsong reigned supreme once more as Jenny drifted
back to sleep.

A week to the day after Buxton arrived at the
hunting box in response to Birdie Pamphrey's
frantic summons, he again invaded his daughter-
in-law's bedchamber. He acknowledged the maid
seated at her bedside with a cool nod before he
transferred troubled eyes to Jenny, presently engaged in peaceful slumber. Though a sennight
had passed, the severe shock he'd sustained when
he'd first laid eyes on her still lingered. Small
wonder. The poor sweet child had looked like a
wraith clinging to life by a gossamer thread. He
gave a mirthless chuckle. And bald as a cue ball
to boot!

To be sure, he'd confronted Jenny's doctor the
very next time he'd crossed the threshold. The
fact that Dr. Ellers was not a cocky young sur-
geon had helped reassure the marquess. That
he'd studied medicine at the august university in
Edinburgh further tipped the scales in his favor.

Even so, Buxton had resolved to leave no stone
unturned in his zeal to insure that his daughter-
in-law received the finest medical care, and if

that meant calling in a London specialist, so be it.

Refusing to be rattled by his lordship's starchiness, Dr. Ellers had parried each query with commendable address.

"My lord, there's no reason to fly into a taking. Lady Temple's baldness is only a temporary aberration."

"Temporary or no, I cannot like it. Surely there must have been something you could have done to stem the tide before she lost every single hair on her head."

"Not to my knowledge. Hair loss is a common occurrence with diphtheria patients. Far more worrisome is the membrane growing in her throat that threatens to close off her air passage."

The marquess had felt the blood drain from his head. "Are you telling me she may die?"

"It's a distinct possibility. Because not only do we have the thick membrane to contend with, the disease could have a dire effect on either her heart or her nervous system. Worst of all, she's running a high fever. Only if it breaks does she stand a chance."

"Good Lord, what's to be done?"

"She already receives the best care possible. I fear her fate's in God's hands." The doctor bowed. "Pray excuse me. I must look in on my patient."

The instant Dr. Ellers took leave of him, Lord Buxton buried his head in his hands. God help him, what had he done? Mind you, at the time he'd sincerely believed he was doing the penniless Miss Shaw a favor by bestowing her hand upon his son and heir. But now, with the benefit of hindsight, he deeply regretted that he'd meddled. Weighed down by guilt, the marquess wondered if he'd ever be able to look himself in the eye again.

A few days later, Buxton returned to the sickroom after an early morning consultation with Jenny's doctor. He ran a shaky hand through his thick thatch of iron gray hair. By Harry, last night had been a near rum go. And even though her fever finally broke just before dawn and even though Dr. Ellers had taken pains to reassure him that the crisis was past, Buxton was almost afraid to believe that Jenny was now on the road to recovery.

Jenny, sensing herself under surveillance, slowly raised her eyelids. How very odd, she thought. Lord Buxton, on whom she hadn't set eyes in over two years, appeared to be sitting in a chair drawn close to her bed. Scarcely able to believe what she saw, she blinked. But when she dared to look again, he was still there. "What? You here, sir?"

"Just so, my lady."

"But why, sir?"

The marquess gave a hearty chuckle. "Wrong season to ride to the hounds, hey what?" When she failed to smile, he sobered. "You've been very ill, child. Birdie sent word."

"How good of you to come all this way."

"Nonsense. I'm delighted to see you finally on the mend. Besides, my visit gives me a chance to get acquainted with little Alexander. I must say I look forward to meeting my grandson, once the doctor says it's safe."

"His brothers, too, I should hope!" Jenny exclaimed tartly.

"Brothers?"

"I refer to the twins, of course."

The marquess's eyes grew round as silver crowns. "Twins?"

Jenny nodded. "Born the seventeenth of April."

"Well, if that don't beat all! What does Andrew have to say about this?"

Her eyes hardened. "I've no idea. Although I wrote him shortly after Aubrey and Alistair were born, he never bothered to respond."

The same month that Jenny wrote Andrew, Napoleon invaded Russia. In London, Silas Minton carefully weighed her request that he forward her letter to her husband. After due deliberation, the solicitor decided that the birth of twin sons—given the fact that the viscount already had an heir—was not of sufficient importance to send Jenny's letter via diplomatic pouch. So he sent it by regular post and grudgingly increased her allowance a smidgen to offset the extra expense of two more mouths to feed.

In normal times, Minton's decision to send the

letter by surface mail would not have delayed delivery above a month. But what with the Grand Army constantly advancing and its Russian counterpart in steady retreat, chaos reigned, and survival, not prompt mail delivery, became a prime objective. Consequently Jenny's letter did not show up until August in St. Petersburg, where it had to be forwarded yet again because the British Embassy had followed the Russian court to Moscow.

On September 14, 1812, Napoleon reached the outskirts of Moscow, and Jenny's letter was delivered to the British Embassy. Andrew's valet ran across it while sorting through the post. Parsons, by nature fastidious, wrinkled his nose in distaste. And to be fair to him, Jenny's letter not only looked as if it had fallen into the mud and then been run over by a mail coach, it had been. Nor were these mishaps the only indignities it had suffered in its circuitous journey.

Parsons tried not to cringe as he gingerly lifted the letter up by the corner he deemed the cleanest and dropped it atop a pile of unopened mail stacked upon a valise he'd packed earlier for their mad dash to St. Petersburg. Truth be told, he was extremely annoyed with his master for volunteering to remain behind to destroy documents deemed too sensitive to be allowed to fall into enemy hands. Every instinct screamed to flee at once. Indeed, the Russian army had already fled. As had the entire British Embassy. With the single exception of Viscount Temple. Who, depending on one's point of view, was either very brave or lamentably bacon-brained. Parsons couldn't decide which.

But while he was contemplating the subject of bacon-brained decisions, Viscount Temple's desertion of his wife and son took top honors. Furthermore, while too proud to admit it, his master had been perfectly miserable ever since he'd left her behind at the hunting box. Not that it was Parson's place to judge his betters. But despite the viscount's brilliant mind, at times he could be remarkably obtuse. Parsons sighed. If only the master had not become so caught up in his ambitions that he'd failed to recognize how much he loved his wife, they need never have come to Russia. Which meant Parsons would not now be quaking in his boots because Boney was on the verge of entering Moscow.

The valet ceased pacing the anteroom floor. He'd like to drag his master out of the Ambassador's office by the scruff off his neck and stuff him into the waiting coach before some enterprising vandal stole it and left them stranded. Fortunately, Parsons, who scarcely weighed nine stone soaking wet, had a healthy regard for his own skin. So instead, he stared resentfully at the connecting door.

On the far side of the door, Andrew stood at the hearth, feeding papers one by one to the greedy flames. As he watched sheet after sheet burn, his thoughts turned inward and an indescribable sadness settled upon him like a shroud. Once again it was September, the month he'd left his wife and son to seek excitement and glamour in the diplomatic milieu.

Expression sardonic, he peered into the mirror above the mantelpiece. His eyes were bloodshot from lack of sleep; his face had the dubious honor of hosting a two-day growth of stubble that itched like the devil. So much for glamour! he chided his reflection.

The truth was, although an entire year had passed since he'd left Jenny behind, he still missed her. The truth was his taste for frivolity had waned, along with his taste for sophisticated beauties bent on dalliance. The truth was with Russia in a state of chaos, his usefulness as a diplomat was moot. The truth was he ached to go home and make his peace with Jenny, but he feared he'd burned his bridges.

Parsons opened the door and slipped quietly into the room. "My lord?"

Turning, Andrew glared at him irritably and asked, "What the devil do you want?"

"Dusk approaches. The vandals grow bolder. If we don't leave now, we may not escape Boney."

Grim-faced, Andrew regarded his valet intently, then gestured toward a pile of papers stacked on the hearth. "That's the last of it."

Parsons's gaze darted toward the papers, considerably cheered to see the pile was less than two inches high. "Then you'll only be a few more minutes?"

"That's right. Why don't you load our things into the coach while I finish up."

"Excellent advice, sir."

Parsons scurried off to do his master's bidding. After stowing their luggage aboard the coach, the valet picked up the stack of unopened mail. In his haste, he missed seeing Jenny's letter slide from the pile and land on the polished marble floor.

Inside the Ambassador's office, Andrew replaced the fire screen and hurried into the anteroom. As he donned his fur-lined overcoat and plunked his fur hat on his head, he noted the travel-soiled letter. Due to its bedraggled appearance, though, it never crossed his mind that the missive he cavalierly kicked aside in his rush to join Parsons might be from Jenny.

A half-hour after Andrew's departure, looters emerged from the shadows to rob and plunder. When they broke into the Embassy, one lit Jenny's letter and used it to torch the drapery. By the time the Grand Army entered Moscow, the entire city was in flames, forcing Napoleon to retire to Petrouski Palace just outside the city, where two days later he wrote Czar Alexander to scold him for leaving the city at the mercy of vandals.

Nine

1813 . . .

Hands clasped behind him, Lord Buxton paced back and forth, a ferocious scowl on his homely face. After a month's visit to Jenny's seaside cottage, where she was still recuperating, he was eager to return to Halpern Abbey. Though lord knew he'd miss both her and his three grandsons once he'd gone. But before he went, he needed to have a serious talk with his daughter-in-law, and he dreaded the outcome. Indeed, if he could, he'd continue to stand mum in regard to the entire tangle, but, unfortunately, such a course was no longer feasible.

Cocking an ear, he recognized Jenny's light tread. His scowl fled, and he turned to face the doorway just as she crossed the threshold.

"You wished to speak to me, sir?"

"Yes, I do. Please sit down. What I have to say may come as something of a shock."

"Don't tell me Sandor's in hot water again. Why, it's barely an hour since breakfast."

Buxton shook his head. "It's not Sandor's be-

havior, nor that of the twins I wish to discuss.
It's Andrew's."

"Andrew's?" Like a cloud hiding the sun, a
shadow darkened hazel eyes to burnished gold.
"In that case, sir, perhaps I will sit down."

"A wise decision, m'dear."

Masking his impatience, the marquess managed
to hold his tongue until she'd seated herself on
the chintz-covered sofa. "Believe me, I'd be
pleased to keep my tongue between my teeth if
I could, but . . ."

Jenny threw up her hands and said with more
than a hint of exasperation, "Lord Buxton, if
you entertain a modicum of fondness for me, you
will quit hemming and hawing and tell me immediately."

"Very well. I wish to discuss a divorce."

She visibly paled. "Andrew wishes to divorce
me?"

Her anguished whisper smote his conscience.
"No, of course not! What I wish to discuss is the
Quinlan divorce."

Jenny stared at him blankly. "The Quinlan divorce, sir?"

The marquess sighed. Getting down to the particulars was going to be harder than he'd envisioned. "Patience, m'dear. I shall explain all. You
see, shortly before your marriage, Andrew became entangled in a love affair with Lady Quinlan. Her husband retaliated by initiating divorce
proceedings, which threatened to wreck my son's
diplomatic career. At that point, I stepped in. I

agreed to use my influence to mitigate the repercussions of the looming scandal if, in return, Andrew would agree to marry you."

Every remaining drop of color drained from Jenny's face. "Dear heaven. So that's why he wed me. How lowering to know the true reason."

Buxton kept a wary eye peeled, sorry now that he'd been so blunt. She was pale as a ghost. Whatever would he do if she swooned?

Jenny gave an anguished moan, then said in a voice tinged with bitterness, "So you are the unseen puppet master pulling the strings. Shame on you, sir."

The marquess raised his right hand as if taking an oath. "As God is my judge, I wish I'd never meddled. But I swear by all that's holy that I thought I was doing both of you a good turn. Can you ever forgive me?"

Jenny stared at him for what seemed to be an interminable length of time. At last she let out an enormous sigh and said, "In view of your many kindnesses, I suppose I must."

"Thank you from the bottom of my heart. It's far more than I deserve, but at least now I can go to my maker with a clean slate."

Jenny shot him a look guaranteed to wither the most promising of blooms. "My lord, there's no call to grow maudlin."

The marquess found her tart rejoinder so amusing, he gave a shout of laughter. Tears of mirth bathed his ruddy cheeks as he said, "M'dear, you are a treasure. But, truth be told, my health is not as stout as I would wish. Which is why I've deeded over this cottage to you in your maiden name. Here, take it."

Mystified, Jenny reluctantly took the scroll of thick parchment he offered.

"Mind you, whether you and Andrew reconcile or not, I believe he'll deal with you fairly. But since I cannot be absolutely certain of this, I've decided to insure that you are left with a measure of independence."

"Most generous of you, sir. However, I am under the impression that anything I own automatically becomes my husband's property."

"In general, that is true. But there are ways of getting around this. Rest assured the cottage is yours all right and tight."

"Thank you. Do you mind if I ask you something?"

"Of course not. What troubles you?"

"Once I got better, I did wonder why you leased the cottage in my maiden name."

"Did you by God? And yet you waited a whole year to ask."

"And now that I have?"

Buxton gave a rueful chuckle. "Allow me to set the scene. At the time I signed the lease, you were still recuperating. I expected Quinlan's suit to be tried any day, and in your weakened state, I feared you might suffer a relapse if confronted with the sordid details of the crim. con. case."

"So you acted out of consideration for my feelings?"

At his nod, Jenny awarded him a peck on the cheek. "What a relief. You see, I thought you used my maiden name on the lease and asked the servants to address me as Mrs. Shaw for an entirely different reason."

"Oh? What other reason if I may be so bold?"

Jenny's eyes mirrored her distress. "I thought you were ashamed to acknowledge the connection."

"By Jove, I see I've much to answer for. Forgive me, Jenny. I never dreamed you'd place such an interpretation on my action. Believe me, I'm proud to call you daughter. My sole motive was to shield you from vicious gossip. Which is why I didn't invite you to make your home with me at Halpern Abbey last autumn."

"Say no more, sir. I quite understand. Indeed, I can think of nothing more distressing than to be an object of scorn."

"Just so. 'Tis now my understanding that the Quinlan case is scheduled to go before Parliament late in January. And since I am certain I can whisk you back here long before then, I wonder if you'd be willing to spend Christmas with me at the Abbey. I would not dream of asking except it's my dearest wish to spend the holidays there with you and my grandsons, and to be brutally frank, my doctor advises me that my health is precarious."

A wry smile enlivened Jenny's features. "Put like that, how can I possibly refuse?"

"You and the boys will join me then?"

"Yes, all of us will come."

Obviously pleased, the marquess was still beaming when Soames, the butler, entered. The marquess had hired him and his wife, who cooked, the previous summer.

"M'lord, your travel coach awaits your pleasure."

Buxton rose to his feet and offered Jenny his arm. He was dangerously short of breath by the time he drew to a halt beside the smart-looking berlin coach waiting to transport him to his principal country seat on the outskirts of Sticklepath. A razor-sharp pain shot up his left arm and spread into his chest cavity, causing him to wince. As the pain gradually dissipated, the marquess recalled his doctor's warning to take life easier. Although impatient to set off, he deliberately took time to admire the autumn foliage, drink in the clean salty tang of the English Channel, watch two gulls wheeling overhead, and listen to the muted roar of the surf as it rolled in to meet the ragged coastline of southern Devon.

He was recalled back to the present by Jenny, who, standing on tiptoe, bestowed a kiss on his florid cheek.

"Hmph. A bit late in the day to try to turn me up sweet, m'dear."

"No such thing, I assure you. The boys and I shall miss you."

The marquess gazed at her fondly. "Fustian! My visit turned your household upside down. And speaking of visits, I'll send my travel coach to fetch you in December. Look for it the week before Christmas."

A footman, resplendent in dark green livery trimmed with gold braid, hopped down from his perch to offer the marquess a steady hand to grip as he mounted the coach steps. However, before his lordship could avail himself, a commotion at the front door of the cottage diverted his attention. The marquess peered at the scene unfolding on the doorstep, the site the eldest of his three grandsons had picked to stage a temper tantrum of the first water.

"Oh dear. I fear Alexander is taking your departure badly. He doesn't want you to leave, you know."

Torn between anger and amusement at his grandson's unseemly display, the marquess snorted. "Someone should inform him that screeching at the top of his lungs is no way to get me to change my mind. On the contrary, it's more likely to speed me on my journey."

Jenny sighed. "I agree he is being very naughty."

Sensing her chagrin, Buxton glanced at Jenny, presently engaged in fanning her rosy cheeks with both hands. "There, there, m'dear, no need to blush."

"Ganfudder!"

The marquess shifted his gaze back to the doorstep just in time to see his sturdy two-and-a-half-year-old grandson wiggle out of the nursemaid's grasp and sprint down the stone steps.

"Ganfudder! Don't go. Stay here wif Sandor!"

Panting for breath, the distraught boy wrapped both arms around one of Buxton's legs.

"Confound it, Sandor, turn me loose!"

The marquess's booming voice was calculated to strike terror in his grandson's heart, but instead of obeying his command, the boy continued to cling to his leg like a tenacious leech. Buxton glared down at his towheaded nemesis with mounting frustration.

Jenny dropped to her knees and cradled her weeping son's head against her breast. The little boy's sobs gradually dwindled to sniffles. Only then was she able to coax him to let go of his grandfather's leg. Rising, she surrendered a now-subdued Alexander to the care of the flustered nursemaid he'd just escaped from and bade her take him to the nursery for his nap. Jenny was still dusting off her skirts as the nursemaid led him inside.

"Sir, please accept my apology for Sandor's behavior."

"To be sure, the little scamp kicked up some dust, but no doubt my departure overset him. But you, m'dear, have no reason to apologize. As usual, your behavior cannot be faulted."

When Jenny lowered her lashes and did not deign to answer, the marquess looked rueful. "Come to that, if anyone ought to apologize, it should be me, not you. Only consider; I leave you at the mercy of three rambunctious toddlers."

Jenny managed a tremulous smile. "Pray do not

refine on it overmuch, my lord. I am more resilient than I appear."

"Just so, m'dear. And thank God for it!"

Her smile widened. "I must admit they are a handful. Fortunately I adore all three of my sons, even when they are up to their ears in mischief."

Eyes twinkling, Buxton awarded her a deep bow before he allowed his footman to assist him into his coach. Jenny waved to him as the vehicle began to pick up speed. Inside the berlin, Buxton kept his eyes trained on her until a bend in the road cut off his view of the cottage, then leaned back against the squabs and lapsed into a brown study.

Though he would have liked nothing better than to board up the cottage and invite Jenny and his three grandsons to make their home with him at his principal seat, the impending divorce case precluded such a course of action. For a year he'd lived in daily expectation that the Quinlan divorce case would soon reach the civil court docket, but it was not until August 1813 that Quinlan finally brought his case before the common law court at King's Bench. Naturally all the sordid details of the affair had been dragged out in public. But now at least the worst hurdle had been crossed.

Even so, he thanked God that his son and heir was still safely abroad, for as he'd anticipated, Andrew had been named the Marchioness of Quinlan's lover. And as the "wronged spouse," Quinlan had been awarded 25,000 pounds monetary damages. A hefty sum to be sure. Yet in hopes of spiking the guns of the tattlemongers, Buxton was eager to shell it out the instant he reached Halpern Abbey.

Vain hopes no doubt, the marquess reluctantly conceded as the carriage bowled along, given the nature of gossips. This factor alone made it impossible for Jenny and the children to spend the autumn months at Halpern Abbey, where her presence could not be kept a secret. Indeed, even inviting her to spend the holidays at the Abbey was taking a calculated risk. But confound it, his health was not as robust as he would like, and he longed to see Jenny firmly established as Viscountess Temple before he went to meet his maker.

To be sure, he'd be obliged to send her back to the seaside cottage right after Boxing Day because, having already been granted a church divorce at Bishop's court as well as a decree from superior court at King's Bench, the Quinlan divorce case was scheduled to be debated in the House of Lords in January. Naturally this event would stir up the scandal all over again, but, God willing, by this time next year, Buxton would finally be able to bring Jenny and his grandsons to live with him at the Abbey—at least part of the year.

Meantime, all four appeared to thrive at the seaside cottage. And even though Jenny had misunderstood his motives, thank God he'd had the foresight to instruct the servants to address her as Mrs. Shaw when he'd leased the cottage the previous summer. For Jenny had suffered enough hurt at the hands of the Halpern family without being subjected to vicious gossip. Indeed, Buxton would not knowingly expose her to any more pain—not if he could help it.

His florid countenance brightened as he pictured Jenny romping on the beach with her three toddlers. When he'd escorted her down the aisle almost three and a half years ago, she'd put him in mind of a newborn colt still unsteady on its feet. A faint smile twitched at the corners of his mouth. Doubtless, he reflected, chasing after his three grandsons had contributed to her newfound grace and agility.

Truth be told, he never ceased to be amazed at the improvement in Jenny's looks. Gone forever was the downy white-blond fluff which had passed for hair before she'd succumbed to diphtheria. And good riddance.

Nowadays, as if her fairy godmother had waved a magic wand, Jenny's bland coloring was a thing of the past. For her new crop of hair had grown in both a different color and texture. Thick curly tresses that after a year's time barely brushed her shoulders were a rich dark honey that admirably set off her creamy complexion. Furthermore, her eyebrows and eyelashes had darkened as well, a factor that called attention to the golden flecks in her hazel eyes.

With a gleeful chuckle, the marquess rubbed his hands together in anticipation of Andrew's reaction the next time he set eyes on Jenny. Indeed, he could hardly wait for his son's return, for Andrew's plump, gauche, young bride had been transformed into a lovely golden swan.

Ten

Goldenrod edged the wheat field undulating in the lazy afternoon breeze. A month had passed since Lord Buxton had returned to Halpern Abbey ostensibly to see to estate matters, but Jenny felt that was only an excuse. She suspected that living the entire month of August in the cramped Devon cottage while at the beck and call of three boisterous grandsons had been a strain on his nerves, and that he'd gone home to get some peace and quiet.

Jenny selected a stick of colored chalk from the wooden box. It was not a perfect match to the goldenrod, but she would just have to make do, since no other piece came close. Today she chose to work with pastels, and as she drew, she could hear the sound of scythes being wielded by farmhands cutting wheat in a nearby field.

She hoped to capture the vivid ochre-colored flower on paper, since to her it epitomized the autumn season. And besides, she wanted to add goldenrod to her collection of wildflower sketches. But as the afternoon advanced, she couldn't seem to concentrate. Indeed, she'd already ruined three pieces of sketching paper. Now her eyes narrowed to slits as she compared her fourth attempt with the live sprig of goldenrod. Discouraged, her shoulders slumped. Whatever was the matter with her? She couldn't seem to draw anything.

Exasperated, Jenny closed the lid of the wooden box. No point in sketching any more today—not in her present unsettled frame of mind. Her eyes clouded. She missed her father-in-law's company. She'd grown quite fond of him during the year since he'd shown up at the hunting box to assume the household reins. A faint smile touched her lips. His blunt manner never failed to ruffle Birdie's feathers, whereas Buxton felt that the nurse's constant fussing over his grandsons would turn them into milksops. Given this clash of wills, Jenny considered it nothing short of amazing that he'd managed to move the entire nursery from a hunting box in Leicestershire to a seashore cottage in Devon. Still, while she was ever so grateful for all he'd done to help speed her recovery, Jenny would be the first to admit they had few interests in common.

But despite this lack, she almost wished her father-in-law were here instead of at the Abbey, because all day long she felt at loose ends. The truth was she was in desperate need of a friend.

Not that she'd ever had any—at least none of longstanding. As a bride, she'd regarded Andrew as her best friend in the world until he'd turned his back on her. And while fond of her father-in-law, his brusque manner and mercurial temper made him, in Jenny's eyes at least, a less-than-ideal confidant.

As for the servants, while they always seemed to know one's business, confiding in them was simply not done. Even Birdie, who in her role of family retainer never hesitated to speak her mind, would be offended if Jenny stepped over the invisible line that separated one class from another.

Nor could Jenny confide in her sons. They were much too young. But even if they were older, it seemed unfair to burden them with her problems and concerns. And, besides, their understanding was limited by their ages, just as their conversation, as a rule, was more repetitious than scintillating.

Nor could she confide in her neighbors, whom she'd never bothered to cultivate, because, living under an assumed name, she'd thought it wise not to mingle socially.

Good thing she liked to sketch so much, Jenny mused glumly. If she couldn't paint and draw, she'd have been at wit's end trying to find a pastime to eat the endless hours spent in her own company. Hours other women spent calling on friends and neighbors.

Today, she felt so blue-deviled she almost wished she'd faced her neighbors instead of retreating into her shell. For while she loved her sons very much, she was lonesome. Too late, she regretted turning away all callers. At present, even the vicar's wife never invited her to call unless the marquess was in residence. And since her father-in-law scorned doing the pretty, Jenny always felt obliged to decline the dubious honor of crossing the parsonage's threshold.

Her expression grew rueful. Actually the person whose company she sorely missed was her husband's. But she wasn't going to think about Andrew. Not if she could help it. Too painful.

She stifled a groan. No wonder she couldn't concentrate today. It was September once again; the month he'd broken her heart by telling her that she had neither beauty nor poise nor sufficient wit to hold his interest; the month he'd ridden off to London without a backward glance. Apparently he'd never regretted his decision since, from that day to this, she'd had no word from him—with the sole exception of the letter he'd written her shortly before he'd set sail.

Jenny's expression grew troubled. By far the worst hurt had occurred during her father-in-law's last visit. Although several weeks had now passed, she still retained a vivid memory of his troubled face when he'd revealed details of the scandal that had raged all summer, unbeknownst to Jenny. He'd feared she'd be angry with him both for resorting to subterfuge the previous summer and for not telling her the truth once she got better. But how could she be angry when it was such a relief to learn that he wasn't ashamed of her? How could she be angry when he'd leased the cottage in her maiden name to insure her peace of mind during her recuperation? How could she be angry when he'd shielded her from the vindictive scorn she'd be subjected to should her neighbors learn her true identity?

Only later, after she'd had a chance to digest all the nuances of the marquess's disquieting revelation, did Jenny wish he'd never told her a thing. Because now that Andrew's true motive for marrying her was out in the open, all her dreams were shattered. Foolish dreams no doubt, yet, they'd sustained her, lifted her when she'd been depressed. And now what did she have? All she had was the cold, steely truth to face. Andrew had never cared two pins for her. What he cared about was his diplomatic career. He'd prized it above all else and had been willing to do whatever was necessary to save it. Even marry homely Jenny Shaw.

How could she have been so blind? She winced as a sharp pain sliced through all her defenses to expose her aching heart. She grimaced in disgust at her naiveté. Unsuspecting fool that she was, she'd fallen in with her father-in-law's scheme without a murmur of protest. Jenny let out a deep sigh. Not that she'd had any other choice. It had been marry his son or starve.

Folding her easel, she stowed it along with her box of pastels and her drawing pad inside the garden shed, then began to meander with no particular destination in mind. As she walked, Jenny sensed a great void in her life that left her

TAKE ADVANTAGE OF THIS SPECIAL OFFER, AVAILABLE *ONLY* TO ZEBRA REGENCY ROMANCE READERS.

You are a reader who enjoys the very special kind of love story that can only be found in Zebra Regency Romances. You adore the fashionable English settings, the sparkling wit, the captivating intrigue, and the heart-stirring romance that are the hallmarks of each Zebra Regency Romance novel.

Now, you can have these delightful novels delivered right to your door each month and never have to worry about missing a new book. Zebra has made arrangements through its Home Subscription Service for you to preview the three latest Zebra Regency Romances as soon as they are published.

3 **FREE** REGENCIES TO GET STARTED!

To get your subscription started, we will send your first 3 books ABSOLUTELY FREE, as our introductory gift to you. NO OBLIGATION. We're sure that you will enjoy these books so much that you will want to read more of the very best romantic fiction published today.

SUBSCRIBERS SAVE EACH MONTH

Zebra Regency Home Subscribers will save money each month as they enjoy their latest Regencies. As a subscriber you will receive the 3 newest titles to preview FREE for ten days. Each shipment will be at least a $11.97 value (publisher's price). But home subscribers will be billed only $9.90 for all three books. You'll save over $2.00 each month. Of course, if you're not satisfied with any book, just return it for full credit.

FREE HOME DELIVERY

Zebra Home Subscribers get free home delivery. There are never any postage, shipping or handling charges. No hidden charges. What's more, there is no minimum number to buy and you can cancel your subscription at any time. No obligation and no questions asked.

TO GET YOUR 3 FREE BOOKS
LL OUT AND MAIL THE COUPON BELOW

Mail to: Zebra Regency Home Subscription Service
120 Brighton Road
P.O. Box 5214
Clifton, New Jersey 07015-5214

YES! Start my Regency Romance Home Subscription and send me my 3 FREE BOOKS as my introductory gift. Then each month, I'll receive the 3 newest Zebra Regency Romances to preview FREE for ten days. I understand that if I'm not satisfied, I may return them and owe nothing. Otherwise, I'll pay the low members' price of just $9.90 for all 3 books and save over $2.00 off the publisher's price (a $11.97 value). There are no shipping, handling or other hidden charges. I may cancel my subscription at any time and there is no minimum number to buy. In any case, the 3 FREE books are mine to keep regardless of what I decide.

NAME		
ADDRESS		APT NO.
CITY	STATE	ZIP
( )		
TELEPHONE		
SIGNATURE	(if under 18 parent or guardian must sign)	**RG0594**

Terms and prices subject to change. Orders subject to acceptance by Zebra Home Subscription Service, Inc.

feeling dissatisfied. Her problem was she had no-body to confide in, nobody to talk to.

She reached the wet strip of sand and turned to walk along the water's edge toward the break-water, a stone wall that arched outward from the shoreline in a semicircle to create a calm harbor for sea traffic.

On rare occasions, she walked from her cottage, located on the outskirts of Torquay, to the town's center. This she did only when she badly needed to purchase an item from the local shops. Even then, although the local tradesmen welcomed her with open arms, she never lingered because she didn't want to risk an awkward confrontation. By and large her neighbors shunned her. Thank goodness. Until the divorce scandal was replaced by another, she dare not reveal her true identity to anyone—not even the vicar.

But even if there had been no impediments to her entering local society, Jenny would have hesi-tated. She'd grown up in Sticklepath and was well-acquainted with the provincial small-minded mentality that flourished in isolated settings. Thus, she'd intuitively known that the town gos-sips could hardly wait to ferret out her exact re-lationship to the Halpern family.

Jenny knew that she couldn't bear to admit to anyone—let alone perfect strangers—that she was married to a man who wanted nothing further to do with her.

A throbbing ache squeezed her heartstrings. Her eyes stung with unshed tears. Dear God, even now, two years after he'd left her, it still hurt to admit Andrew's poor opinion of her. But to pursue that tangent was fruitless. Far better to concern herself with the present.

Jenny paused to admire a cluster of white rock-rose prevalent in Devon, especially in autumn. Fortunately she had her genuine interest in botany to fall back on. Much as she treasured the hours she spent with her sons, there were times when she thought if she were denied adult conversation a minute longer, she'd go mad. Happily, too, drawing had ever been a favorite pastime. Why, in the past year alone, she'd completed an impressive number of sketches of native wildflowers that grew near Devon's southern coastline to add to the collection she'd started in Leicestershire. Today she'd been all thumbs, but normally, once engrossed, she forgot all her troubles.

But now it was September once more, the month when her bouts of melancholy were most severe. Despite Andrew's cavalier treatment of her, not only did she still love him, in her secret heart of hearts, she knew she'd love him as long as she lived.

Jenny continued her ramble until an ominous clap of thunder prompted her to cast a worried glance at the sky. The sun had ducked behind the bank of dense gray clouds while she'd been too preoccupied to notice. A flash of lightning followed by a patter of raindrops persuaded her to focus on her present predicament. Unhappily she'd strayed too far from the cottage to reach it in time to prevent a thorough soaking.

She glanced about seeking shelter. To her dismay, she recognized no landmarks. Foolishly she'd wandered farther afield than ever before.

A second flash of lightning revealed a gazebo only a short distance away. Lifting her skirts high enough so she wouldn't trip, she raced up the wooden steps, but a pelting sheet of hard raindrops managed to saturate her thin muslin gown before she could gain shelter under the gazebo's roof.

"Upon my word, young woman, you're soaked to the skin."

Jenny took a moment to get her bearings before she hazarded a peek at her sodden dress. The thin muslin material clung to her skin. What a quiz she must look to the stately presence eying her with candid interest.

"Indeed, ma'am, I venture to say I bear a close resemblance to a drowned rat."

The woman laughed. "Never mind. Provided we get you warm and dry without delay, you should suffer no harm."

Rising, she transferred all the dishes from the table onto a silver tray, which she set on the floor. Next, she plucked the linen cloth off the table and presented it to Jenny.

"Here. Use this to dry off."

Jenny wiped her face and arms with the tablecloth while taking surreptitious peeks at the woman, who appeared to be in her early fifties.

While her coal black hair contained streaks of silver, she was blessed with patrician features that seemed ageless. Indeed, Jenny couldn't help but wonder if she were even more handsome in her maturity than she had been in her youth. For certain her satiny complexion appeared untouched by the ravages of time, with the exception of faint laugh lines that fanned from the corners of piercing blue eyes. Jenny welcomed those telltale crinkles because they indicated that she loved to laugh. And if anyone needed cheering up, it was her hostess's sodden guest.

She was wringing excess moisture from her sopping wet hair when her hostess next spoke. "The downpour should cease in a trice. Be ready to make a mad dash to my bungalow. Once there, I can promise a hot bath and a change of clothes."

Jenny smiled. "That sounds heavenly. But I hate to impose."

"Rubbish! I'm stuck here in the country until my troublesome cough is vanquished. Doctor's orders. And to be frank, I was about to succumb to a fatal case of ennui before you showed up."

Jenny stared at the woman, not quite sure whether she ought to trust her cheerful demeanor. Her would-be benefactress gave a trill of laughter.

"My dear, I hope we shall become friends. By the by, I am Maybelle, the Dowager Duchess of Dillon. And you are?"

"Jenny Halpern, Lady Temple, ma'am." Jenny

was halfway through her curtsy when she felt her complexion turn beet red. "Curse my runaway tongue. Your Grace, I must beg you to keep my true identity confidential. I'm known hereabouts as Mrs. Shaw."

The Duchess of Dillon's eyes grew needle-sharp. "What's this? Do you claim to be that notorious rake's wife?"

Jenny managed a painful swallow. Why, oh why, had she opened her mouth? "I fear so, ma'am. However, for the sake of my sons, I beg you to disregard my title and address me by my maiden name or, if you prefer, as Jenny."

"How very diverting! Naturally I quite understand your need to maintain your anonymity in the face of the juiciest crim. con. case in years. So allow me to allay your fears. I give you my solemn word that I shall never betray your secret."

The sincerity in the duchess's voice rang true in Jenny's ears. With a relieved sigh, she uttered her thanks and would have gladly elaborated much longer on that theme if Her Grace hadn't cut her off.

"That's quite enough flummery, child," the duchess insisted. "But come. The rain has momentarily slackened. We must fly if we hope to outrace the next cloudburst."

Once inside the sprawling bungalow, Jenny gratefully warmed herself at the glowing hearth while she waited for a room to be readied for her use.

"Your Grace, there is no need for you to wait, too."

"I wouldn't dream of deserting a newfound friend."

Friend? The term that tripped so easily off the duchess's tongue brought tears to Jenny's eyes. To have a loyal friend would be beyond wonderful. But how could she be certain the duchess was as trustworthy as she seemed? True, she found Her Grace's candor reassuring. Nonetheless, Jenny felt it was too soon in the budding relationship to entirely relax her guard.

"Tell me, my dear, how is it our paths never crossed? Did you not have a Season?"

"No, ma'am. I was only seventeen when I married my husband, and the following spring our son Alexander was born. Then, shortly after my nineteenth birthday, Andrew left me."

"The scoundrel! But, my dear, I thought I understood you to say 'sons' in the plural, or am I laboring under a misunderstanding?"

Jenny's complexion turned a delicate pink. "Sons in the plural is correct, Your Grace. I gave birth to identical twins the following May, seven months after Andrew resumed his diplomatic career."

"What? Do you mean to say your husband deserted you when you were *enceinte*?"

The duchess's scowl was so fierce, Jenny almost cringed. Still in all, it would hardly be fair to paint her husband's character blacker than it actually was.

"To do him justice, at the time of his departure, Andrew had no inkling that I was in a family way."

The duchess regarded her shrewdly. "And you, my dear? Did you not guess that you were in a delicate condition?"

Jenny's eyes swam with hot tears. Angry with herself, she refused to let a single teardrop fall. "Credit me with some pride. Had I told him, he might have stayed on until their birth, but that would have only postponed the inevitable."

"You believe he does not care for you at all then?"

"His feelings toward me are at best lukewarm. The problem is I love him anyway. That's why it hurts that I cannot even command his respect—let alone earn his love."

"Fiddle-faddle! If you truly care, then you should not have given up so easily. You should have channeled all your efforts into encouraging him to love you back."

"So I thought, ma'am. At least I did until . . ."

"Until?" the duchess echoed in an encouraging manner.

Jenny swallowed the tears clogging her throat. "Until Andrew made it quite clear that he wished to return to the diplomatic circles and that he saw me as a stone around his neck in that milieu. Even after he'd insulted me, I swallowed my pride and begged him to teach me how to go on. Believe me, Your Grace, I was eager to learn what-

ever he deemed necessary, but he spurned my
offer and refused to give me a chance."

"Well, of all the shabby creatures, Andrew
Halpern takes the palm! But never you mind, my
dear. I shall personally take you under my wing,
and once I've finished polishing your rough
edges, I dare swear that insufferable peacock will
soon change his tune. So when do we start?"

"Are you perfectly serious?" Jenny asked doubt-
fully.

"Most emphatically."

"In that case, why not immediately?"

"Famous! But first thing tomorrow morning
ought to be soon enough. Now then, here is one
of the upstairs maids to see to your room. Inci-
dentally, dinner has been set back to give us time
to make ourselves presentable."

An hour later, Jenny rejoined the duchess in
the drawing room. She'd had a long soak in a
tub of hot water before Her Grace's dresser arrived to hurry her into one of her mistress's
gowns and to style her hair.

The duchess beamed her a placating smile.
"Now that you're dry and cozy, I feel safe in con-
fessing that I dispatched a footman to your cottage to inform your staff that you will be
spending the night."

"Oh, but, ma'am, I really shouldn't stay. I always read my sons a bedtime story."

"Your devotion to your offspring is admirable,
but surely they can manage to do without your
presence for one night."

"Perhaps you are right, Your Grace, but . . ."

The duchess straightened her spine. "My dear, I absolutely insist that you not stir from this bungalow until morning. Indeed, it is too bad of you to suggest otherwise after all the trouble I've gone to to prevent you from catching a chill."

Jenny noted the duchess's wry expression and the teasing twinkle in her piercing blue eyes.

She burst out laughing. "Very well, Your Grace, you win."

"Excellent. And now do sample the crayfish. Fresh caught today, they fairly melt in your mouth." She motioned a footman to serve her guest.

"Indeed, they look delicious, Your Grace," Jenny agreed. "But I'm too full to do them justice."

The duchess laughed. "I see that I must take care not to ride roughshod over you, else I shall be put sweetly but firmly in my place. And while we are on the subject of not treading on each other's toes, pray let us dispense with so many 'Your Graces?' Do call me Maybelle and I shall call you Jenny, if I may be so bold?"

"I have no objection, ma'am."

"Famous. Now we may be perfectly comfortable."

Jenny smiled, content to let the duchess have the last word. A bubble of happiness rose up inside her. Obviously winning Andrew's love was a lost cause. But at least she'd finally found a friend.

Eleven

One of the marquess's outriders let down the coach steps and helped Jenny to alight before he raced ahead to raise the knocker affixed to the front door of the Duchess of Dillon's sprawling bungalow. Just as Jenny reached that portal, it swung open to reveal the duchess's butler, who motioned her inside.

"Good day, Thornton. Is Her Grace in to callers?"

"Before I inquire, may I take your wrap?"

Glancing down at her oversized sealskin muff, she replied, "No, thank you," as she gazed into the cheval mirror above the carved mantelpiece. "I shan't be staying above ten minutes."

It pleased her that her Regency hat of black sealskin was still tilted at a rakish angle. Color stole into her cheeks. Good heavens! This was no time to be caught primping. She spun round to face the butler.

Thornton bowed. "Then I shall ascertain Her Grace's wishes."

However, before he could begin his ponderous retreat, Jenny darted past him and called back over her shoulder, "No need to bestir yourself,

Thornton. I am in too much of a hurry to stand on ceremony and shall announce myself."

Jenny found her quarry in the morning room seated on a silk brocade sofa. She curtsied. "Good morning, Maybelle."

The magazine the duchess had been thumbing slipped through her fingers, sliding down the front of her royal blue morning gown—cut from a bolt of fine merino wool—and eventually coming to rest on the Brussels carpet.

Jenny rushed forward to retrieve the magazine and hand it back to her hostess. "Forgive me, ma'am. I did not mean to startle you."

"Well, you did all the same! But never mind. You look as fine as fivepence. Is this the habit I goaded you into buying?"

Jenny made a wry face. "You know it is, you dreadful tyrant."

Initially she'd been highly incensed by the duchess's meddling. Her Grace had had the audacity to write Lord Buxton and beg him to advance the necessary funds to provide his daughter-in-law with a wardrobe suitable for a viscountess. Generous to a fault, the marquess had posted a bank draft to cover expenses.

"I'm sorry I made such a fuss initially. Had you not interceded on my behalf, I should have nothing *au courant* to wear on my journey."

"Handsomely said, my dear Jenny. But where are my manners? Have a chair. And once you are comfortable, tell me where you're bound before I die of curiosity."

Maybelle's question reminded Jenny of the grave reason for her journey, and her demeanor sobered. She'd prefer to remain standing, but to ignore the duchess's invitation would seem ungracious. Jenny selected a straight-back chair, where she sat perched as if about to take flight.

"Very well. But first allow me to apologize for bursting in on you unannounced."

The duchess responded with a tinkling laugh. "All you interrupted was a scanning of the October issue of *La Belle Assemblée*. Care for a peek?"

Sad-eyed, Jenny shook her head. "I merely dropped by to bid you adieu. Yesterday I received word that my father-in-law is quite ill. Then, bright and early this morning, his coach arrived to convey me to Halpern Abbey."

"Such unhappy news! I understood Buxton to be in robust health."

"So he was until quite recently. However, two months ago, during his last visit, I found his shortness of breath worrisome. Also, I couldn't help but notice the way the boys got on his nerves."

"I quite understand your anxiety, but surely you have time for a dish of tea before you go."

"Truly, I do not. But I do have a favor to ask."

"Ask away. Anything in my power, I shall happily grant."

"It's Sandor," Jenny confessed. "He likes to scramble over the boulders that form the breakwater, and, since he is remarkably surefooted, I saw no harm in it until recently."

Jenny shuddered at the recollection of Sandor's narrow escape. "It was a good thing I was standing right next to him when he stepped on a patch of wet seaweed. His feet slipped out from underneath him. Luckily I was able to grab hold of him before he tumbled into the sea."

"What a beastly experience!"

Jenny continued, "Neither Sandor nor I can swim a stroke. I have nightmares. I keep seeing his head disappear underwater and wake up in a cold sweat.

"I've voiced my concerns to Birdie. Still, Sandor is famous for twisting her round his finger. I've forbidden him his precious boulders, but with me gone, he may be tempted to disobey. Your Grace, I realize it's a great deal to ask, but would you see that Birdie keeps him off the breakwater during my absence?"

"Of course I will. Do not fret about Sandor or your twin cubs. I promise to keep an eye on them."

With fluid grace, Jenny rose. She smoothed the fingers of kid gloves dyed to match her stone-colored habit, the latter trimmed in swansdown and ornamented across the bosom with row after row of silk braiding. Expression pensive, she permitted herself a fleeting, albeit wry, smile. Birdie would not be pleased to have the Duchess of Dillon poke her nose in what she regarded as her exclusive domain. Coward that she was, Jenny was almost glad she'd be gone when the sparks began to fly.

In anticipation of her protégée's imminent departure, Maybelle advanced with her arms outstretched. She enveloped her friend in a bear-hug.

Once the duchess's arms fell away, Jenny took two steps backward and said, "I really must go."

"Run along then. Mind you'll be sorely missed, so hurry back."

Two days later, a freezing rainstorm accompanied by gale-force winds raged as the marquess's berlin pulled up before the front entrance of Halpern Abbey. Jenny peered out the coach window and shivered. Not only was it dark as pitch outside, it was Allhallows Eve, and, bathed in the pale moonlight, the courtyard looked absolutely frightening. Yet obviously she was expected, because no sooner had one of the outriders helped her to alight than a member of the house staff popped up at her elbow with an umbrella. He introduced himself as James Fielding, his lordship's steward. After he gallantly positioned the umbrella to shield Jenny from the worst of the storm's fury, they dashed across the flagstones.

Once inside the Abbey, Jenny begged news of the marquess's present state of health. Fielding informed her that his lordship still did poorly. He advised her to visit his bedchamber before she retired, since Buxton would be unlikely to get a wink of sleep until assured she'd arrived safe and sound. She followed the steward to the threshold of the master suite, where they were met by Buxton's valet.

Morris had the lean, hungry look of a starved scarecrow and an aura of fatalistic doom that clung to him like a made-to-order shroud. Jenny stifled a shudder. For the life of her, she could not imagine how the marquess tolerated such a gloomy servant.

A crack of thunder jerked her back to the present. She approached the bed where Buxton sat propped upright with the aid of a mound of pillows. His emaciated appearance came as such a shock, Jenny had to work to keep her face blank.

"By Jove, you came," he rasped.

Never in her life had Jenny felt less like smiling. Yet somehow or other, she managed to dredge one up. "Of course I did. I intend to take care of you, just as you did when I was ill."

"Splendid. Now that you're here, maybe I can get a decent night's rest." And so saying, he closed his eyes.

Her second visit to her father-in-law's bedchamber took place the next morning. Noting his improved appearance, Jenny felt a tremendous surge of relief.

"Sir, you look to be in plump currant."

Buxton chuckled. "Slept like a log. Right after breakfast, the local quack honored me with a flying visit. Said if I continue to go on like this, I'll soon be in prime twig."

"Excellent news."

"So it is. At the moment, my spirits are so elevated that not even Morris's morose phiz can dampen them. Sit down, child, and let us catch up on things.''

Jenny was glad that she had at least that opportunity to speak to him, for at dusk the marquess took a turn for the worse and was allowed no visitors. And even though a maid was dispatched to roust Jenny out of her fitful sleep in the middle of the night, Lord Buxton wheezed his last breath before she could reach his bedside. Heartsore, Jenny gently closed his eyes, then laid her weary head upon his broad chest and wept until she had no tears left.

Upon regaining her composure, she thought to rejoin her three sons in Torquay. However, Fielding soon convinced her it was her duty to stay on at the Abbey until after the funeral was over and the will was read.

Jenny knew Fielding was right to insist, but she was reluctant to linger. What if Andrew decided to attend his father's funeral? She could just imagine how vexed he'd be, should he find the wife he'd scorned running tame at Halpern Abbey. However, when she raised the point with Fielding, he assured her that Andrew could never receive the letter in time to attend last rites.

Consequently, it was mid-November before she embarked on her return journey to the seaside cottage she now regarded as her home. The day of her departure dawned clear and crisp, and, thanks to a cold snap that froze the roadbed solid, the coachman was able to make excellent time.

The frosty weather held steady for the entire journey, but since the interior of the berlin coach contained all the luxuries befitting a peer of the realm, including a charcoal brazier to keep toes warm and toasty, Jenny traveled in comfort. Mentally, however, the unseen road she traveled was pockmarked with potholes just waiting to trip her up.

Troubled, Jenny glanced out the coach window. She could scarcely see anything because her vision was blurred by tears. She daubed her eyes, though, and resolutely squared her shoulders. Lord Buxton's sudden death depressed her spirits. But as the travel coach approached the outskirts of Torquay, she realized for the children's sake, if not hers, she must somehow come to terms with her grief.

A week later, Soames entered the cottage's morning room to announce the Duchess of Dillon, who blithely sailed across the threshold.

"Maybelle. How good of you to call." Catching the retreating butler's eye, Jenny ordered a pot of tea.

"Ha! Be thankful that I curbed my impatience long enough to give you a chance to catch your breath."

Trust Her Grace to rush her fences. Smiling, Jenny begged her to be seated.

The duchess settled herself on the end of the couch closest to Jenny's chair.

"My dear, I am on pins and needles. I demand you tell all."

"My father-in-law died," Jenny said soberly.

"I know, my dear, and I am sorry. I read his death notice in the *London Post*. Besides, why else would you be wearing black?"

Why else indeed? Jenny thought. "But if you already knew, why quiz me?"

"Dearest, what I crave are details. Namely, did that errant husband of yours show up?"

Jenny shook her head. "I feared he would, though. I did not take the harsh Russian winters into account."

"Or the war-torn country Napoleon left in the wake of his retreat, I make no doubt. I gather you saw no point in delaying the funeral on the off chance that the new Lord Buxton might arrive in time for last rites."

"Exactly so! It fell to me to greet those members of the local gentry who came to pay their last respects since, other than his son, Lord Buxton had no close relatives on either side of his family."

The duchess cast her a reassuring smile. "I collect you behaved just as you ought. Your father-in-law would be pleased if he knew."

Jenny looked wistful. "Do you truly think so, ma'am?"

"Of a certainty. Why, he could not have been fonder of you if you were his own daughter." Her Grace's demeanor grew shrewd. "And the will? Were you present when it was read?"

At Jenny's nod, the duchess appeared vexed by the paucity of her response. "At the risk of seeming odiously prying, did Lord Buxton provide for you in his will?"

"Yes. He set up a trust fund to take care of the boys' education as well as a small annuity for me. Was that not kind of him, ma'am?"

"Most kind. But will you have enough funds to manage?"

"I think so. In addition to the annuity, Andrew provides me with a quarterly allowance."

"And the combined sum is enough to cover both rent and household expenses?"

"It does not stretch that far. But I need not pay rent. Lord Buxton deeded the cottage over to me in August."

"Did he? How odd." The duchess looked at her curiously.

"Odd? Not really. He knew that I've found a measure of peace and tranquillity here."

"To be sure, but why not leave it to you in his will?"

"Oh, that's no mystery. He feared if he mentioned it there, Andrew might attempt to countermand his wishes. To further muddy the waters, he deeded the cottage to Mrs. Shaw—as I'm known in these parts—not to Viscountess Temple, due to the Quinlan scandal.

"It saddens me to think that he died bitterly disappointed in his son's behavior. Indeed, if I had tuppence for the times that my father-in-law blustered, 'Let Andrew search high and low for you and Sandor. Perhaps he'll come to appreciate what is not so easy to find,' I am persuaded I'd be rich as Croesus.''

"Mercy. Lord Buxton seemed a perfect lamb. Who would have dreamed he had a vindictive streak."

Jenny sighed. "I must admit he was always very kind to me, but I don't believe he and his son were ever close. I regret, though, being the reason Buxton felt antipathy toward Andrew."

"Through no fault of your own. In my opinion, that husband of yours has much to answer for."

"Oh, I agree. And since I can't seem to stop loving him, it's probably best that our paths don't cross anytime soon. However, when Sandor reaches school age, I'm honorbound to inform Andrew of our whereabouts."

"But, Jenny, even assuming your husband doesn't care for you, what makes you think he's willing to wait several more years to see his son?"

"We discussed this matter before he left me. He promised to leave Sandor exclusively in my care until he reaches school age. I imagine Andrew thinks I'm still at the hunting box. Assuming he ever bothers to think of me at all." Jenny's mouth thinned to an angry line.

"So Andrew has no idea you're in Torquay?" the duchess asked.

"No. When Lord Buxton removed the children and me from the hunting box, he was careful to cover our tracks. He even took the precaution of engaging an agent to handle my business affairs. He then instructed Andrew's solicitor to forward my quarterly allowance to my agent's London address, instead of to the bank in Melton as he'd done formerly. So, you see, I am perfectly safe for the next few years so long as I live a quiet life."

"Quiet life?" the duchess sputtered. "Never say so! T'would ruin all my plans."

"Plans, Your Grace? Kindly explain."

Maybelle looked decidedly unhappy. "I so wanted to introduce you to London society in the spring. Surely you wish to cut a dash."

"Who me, ma'am? I cannot imagine where you got that notion."

Thoroughly disgruntled, the duchess narrowed her blue eyes to pinpoints. "Can you not? Do you mean to say all those hours I spent coaching you were for naught?"

In the face of the duchess's sarcasm, Jenny struggled to keep her own voice temperate. "While I've no wish to contradict you, that is simply not true. Indeed, without your training to bolster my confidence, I daresay I'd never have screwed up the courage to play the gracious lady to those who showed up at the Abbey to pay their last respects."

"Fustian! Do you actually think I spent every spare minute teaching you just so you'd feel comfortable entertaining country bumpkins? You disappoint me, Jenny. I thought you had more bottom."

Jenny felt sick to her stomach. Maybelle's friendship meant the world to her. What if Her Grace was so disgusted with her timidity that she decided to cut the connection?

"My dear ma'am, if I mislead you, I humbly beg your pardon. But even assuming I agreed to go along with your plan, the coming Season is out of the question."

"Merely because you are in mourning? Nonsense! Of course, you may not dance, but otherwise you may partake of the delights the Season offers, within reason, of course."

"It still would not do, Duchess. The Quinlan divorce case is scheduled to go before the House of Lords in January."

"Botheration! I must admit I failed to consider that aspect. Still, if I wait until mid-Season to fire you off, the talk will have died down. Besides, if I introduce you as Mrs. Shaw, I daresay any potentially embarrassing incidents would be entirely avoided."

Jenny shook her head. "Maybelle, I just don't have the heart for it. 'Tis too soon after my father-in-law's death."

The duchess sighed. "Perhaps you'll feel up to making your bow during the Little Season?"

"Perhaps. But that's almost a year away. Now is much too soon to decide."

"Yes, that is true. Very well. I will agree to drop the subject of your debut for the present, if you will promise to keep an open mind in regard to a future date."

Smiling, Jenny grumbled, "Your Grace drives a hard bargain, but you have my word."

Twelve

Inside Bellamy's Chop and Coffee House, Andrew Halpern, 8th Marquess of Buxton, sprawled on a Windsor chair. Seated on the opposite side of a table that held the remains of their supper was Lord Piers Shelwyn, a bosom bow since Oxford.

"More hair of the dog?" Shelwyn asked facetiously.

Andrew grinned. "Why not?"

He slid his mug across the table toward his crony. Shelwyn refilled it and sent it back. Andrew lifted the mug and treated himself to a long swallow.

"Ah." He gave a long sigh. "Nothing compares to a mug of English ale. Don't you agree?"

He plunked the half-full mug down on the plank table with such force, a few drops of ale sloshed over the rim.

"I do if you mean Bruton's."

"Doubtless the cream of the crop. But, actually, I had no particular ale in mind. They all taste bloody wonderful after two and a half years abroad." From his waistcoat pocket, Andrew pulled out a handkerchief and wiped off the froth from his upper lip. "Excellent meal."

"Good English fare is what makes this place so popular with our legislatures."

Andrew laughed. "Really? Since Bellamy's adjoins the House of Commons, surely convenience is a factor."

"Proximity certainly doesn't hurt," Shelwyn agreed. "Still, I'll stick to my guns. It's the food."

"Well, I can hardly disagree—not when I've already praised the dish I ordered. But don't forget, I was a trifle sharp set."

Shelwyn snorted. "Sharp set? For a while there, I worried you might gobble me up along with your dinner."

Andrew chuckled. "God knows I'm not usually such a glutton. But after enduring five solid hours of close questioning by Liverpool, I'd begun to wonder if he planned to starve me to death."

"No doubt he was anxious for a firsthand report on the Russian court."

"You couldn't be more mistaken. Liverpool don't give a tinker's damn about Russia. Particularly not when the czar isn't there, but rather in Paris stirring up mischief. Besides, I left St. Petersburg last November bound for Frankfurt, where I hooked up with Castlereagh. The foreign secretary's report is what interests the prime minister. Why, the instant I met him, Liverpool pounced on me like a rat terrier eager to shake every last drop of information out of me. Never mind that a great deal has happened since I left our allies haggling over terms of the peace treaty in Frankfurt."

"Including Bonaparte's abdication," Shelwyn agreed in a voice tinged with dry amusement.

Andrew grinned. "I daresay none of us will know what to do with ourselves now that we are finally at peace."

"Little wonder, after over twenty years of war," Shelwyn responded.

"I will say again, it's good to be back on English soil for a change."

"And your plans for the future?"

Andrew sobered. "First, mend my fences. Second, take on the responsibilities I inherited along with the title. You know, of course, that my father died six months ago."

"Yes. My belated condolences, Andy."

"Thank you. The letter informing me of his death reached St. Petersburg after I'd gone. It didn't catch up with me in Frankfurt until a month after the funeral."

"No wonder you did not attend."

"Just so. One of the drawbacks of the diplomatic career is that you can be assigned to a new post with little warning."

"No great matter. Your father would have understood."

Andrew's brow furrowed. "I wish I could be sure of that. My conscience gnaws at me, Piers."

"Why? Even if you'd stayed in Russia, you still wouldn't have been able to get home in time."

"You are right, of course." He ran a hand through his black curls. "But enough of my troubles. I've scarce seen hide nor hair of you since you married the Toast of the Season and retired with her to your country estate in Sussex. So tell me, Piers, how do you fare?"

His blond friend smiled. "It has been a deuced long time since our paths crossed, has it not? Over four years, I collect. But to answer your question, you see before you an extremely contented husband and father."

"Father? You have children?"

"Yes, a three-year-old daughter and another child on the way. Which is why Eleanor did not accompany me this trip. The happy event is tentatively scheduled sometime in May, and we both felt it was too close to risk it."

"You hope for an heir this time?"

"That would be nice, but so long as dearest Eleanor and the babe come through the ordeal in sound health, I promise you I shall count my blessings."

"You love her still after five years of marriage?"

"More each day that passes. And miss her every minute we're apart. But you, too, have married and sired a child. A son, if I'm not mistaken." Shelwyn's green eyes twinkled.

"Yes, Alexander was three in February, but I've

not seen him since he was six months old. So we shall meet as strangers."

"And your wife? I imagine she's in the alts now that you have come home for good."

"I hardly think so, old chap. Ours is a marriage of convenience."

"Oh, I see. Pity that."

Andrew shrugged. "Not everyone has your phenomenal luck, Piers. My father insisted I wed her. At the time, he was up in the boughs about the scandalous crim. con. case I stupidly blundered into, and he hoped to throw sand in Quinlan's eyes. Didn't work. Not only did Quinlan go through with the divorce, he took his own sweet time getting it. When I left for Russia, he'd just received the church decree from Bishop's court.

"Then, after an entire year passed and Quinlan made no move to press on with the case, both father and I began to hope that he'd be content with a legal separation. But no such luck."

"Hard lines, Andy. It was fortunate his civil suit did not reach the King's Bench docket until last summer when most of the *ton* had forsaken London for Brighton. Of course, the fact that you were safely abroad during the worst of the mudslinging was a blessing. And you can count yourself lucky that your father was so prompt to pay Quinlan the 25,000 pounds the court awarded him. Had he procrastinated, he might have died before he took care of it, and then where would you be?"

"Easy enough to guess. I'd be fair game for

every gossipmonger in London. Indeed, as things stand at the moment, none of my peers at White's seemed overjoyed when I popped in there this afternoon. Only you had the guts to acknowledge me, Piers."

"Andy, there's no need to dump the butter boat over my head. Besides, I don't think they meant to censure your conduct. No one gave you the cut direct, did they?"

"No. Still they were dashed unsociable."

"No doubt because they haven't seen you in ages."

"You may well be right. Besides, it hardly matters since I don't plan to linger in Town now that I've reported to Liverpool on Castlereagh's behalf. I leave tomorrow for Leicester to visit both wife and son."

The hackney cab made the seventh full circuit around Berkeley Square, then ground to an abrupt halt. Jenny heard the driver scramble down from his box and waited with mounting agitation for him to draw level with the cab's open window.

"Why did you stop? I gave no such order."

"Me 'ead be spinnin'. So 'less yer ready to squeak as to where yer goin', kindly 'oppit."

Poor jarvey. She'd worn his patience to a thread. Jenny shot him a placating smile. "Why do you think I told you to keep circling? I cannot make up my mind where I want to be set down.

Please, just one more circuit. Afterward, if I still cannot decide, you may drive me back to the Clarendon."

The jarvey threw up his hands. "Blood and 'ouns! All right, yer ladyship, one more turn. Any more and I'll be gawdelpus," he grumbled.

As the horses drawing the carriage clip-clopped upon the cobblestones, Jenny took herself firmly in hand. No more shilly-shallying. Since she was already in Berkeley Square, it made sense to narrow her choices down to two: Gunter's or the Duchess of Dillon's town house.

Gunter's was renowned for its ices. Jenny was eager to try one but didn't know if a lady entering the august establishment without an escort would be frowned upon. Anyway, Maybelle would be livid if she didn't call on her first, Jenny conceded as the hackney once again approached the duchess's elegant brownstone. And rightly so. For how could she even consider placing indulgence of her sweet tooth on the same plane as their friendship? Mind made up, Jenny tapped on the roof to signal the driver that she wished to be set down.

From the sidewalk, she addressed the driver. "Do you care to wait for me or would you prefer I pay you off?"

"Iffen it be all the same to yer ladyship, I'll take me fare and shab off."

Soon after Jenny lifted the knocker, Thornton responded. He ushered her into the presence of the duchess, who ordered tea and a plate of macaroons before he retreated.

After it came, Maybelle poured the steaming brew into a china cup and handed it to Jenny. "My dear, what a lovely surprise. Dare I think you've undergone a change of heart?"

"I gather you mean in regard to making my bow to society under your kind auspices?"

"Exactly so."

Jenny looked exasperated. "Really, ma'am, must you keep harping on that string?"

"Sheath your claws, child. What else am I to think when I find you on my doorstep at the height of the Season?"

Embarrassed, Jenny flushed. "I beg your pardon, Your Grace. In your shoes, no doubt I'd jump to the same conclusion."

"Quite," the duchess said thinly.

"I promise you the current Season did not lure me to Town; personal business did."

"Pertaining to Buxton's will, I collect?"

"No, ma'am. An entirely different matter."

Maybelle arched an eyebrow. "Are you fencing with me, Jenny?"

"No, indeed, Duchess. 'Tis merely that I am uncertain as to where to start."

"Fustian! Jump in anyplace before I die of curiosity."

Jenny laughed. "Very well. Shortly after my father-in-law's death, you asked me if the annuity he left me was enough to support myself and my three sons. I then confided that I received a quarterly allowance from Andrew and that a combination of the two would insure that I do not outrun the constable."

"But now you've had second thoughts? Perchance you are in Town to badger your husband's man of business into increasing your allowance?"

"Gracious, no. I've too much pride to haggle with that miserly nip cheese."

"Pride won't fill the larder," the duchess admonished gently.

"True! However, shortly after we discussed my solvency, I realized that, while the funds allotted me would cover the necessities, there would be precious little left over to spend on an occasional treat for the boys or to meet unforeseen expenses. Also, ever since Andrew deserted me, I've longed to accomplish something entirely on my own. And now that I have, I can afford to crow a little."

The duchess frowned. "Jenny, I trust you've not done something that will place you beyond the pale."

"I hardly think so, but shall allow you to be the judge."

"How flattering to be sure. But, my dear, you have me at a disadvantage. Do tell me precisely what you've accomplished."

Jenny smiled. "As you wish. I added a text explaining each plant's characteristics to each of my wildflower sketches and submitted the entire manuscript to a reputable London publisher."

"Reputable? How could you evaluate the firm's reputation while stuck in the country?"

"Simple enough. I wrote to my man of business in London and instructed him to make inquiries and then draw up a list. In January, I sent my manuscript to the name at the top and sat back to await results. A sennight ago, I received a letter from J. Brownnell informing me he wished to publish my botany sketchbook. So, now that I've explained my purpose, I trust you understand I did not come to London to become a social butterfly. I came so I could negotiate the terms of my contract in person before I signed it."

Her Grace stared at her mutely.

"Cat got your tongue? I did not mean to shock you."

"Nor have you. Which is not to say I am not rather startled. Why, for a moment there you rendered me speechless. However, I must say I am terribly proud of you."

A radiant glow warmed Jenny from head to toe.

"But what can I be thinking of to be nattering like this? You must be tired from your journey. I'll ring for the housekeeper and order her to prepare you a bedchamber."

"My dear ma'am, that is not at all necessary. I've already taken a room at the Clarendon."

"A hotel? Never say so. Why didn't you call on me the instant you arrived?"

"It was after dark before the afternoon stage set me down at the coaching house. I didn't wish to impose. And this is the first social call I've made."

"I see. And are you quite comfortable at the Clarendon?"

"Indeed, I am. Last night's dinner was my first taste of French cuisine."

"I feel certain it was a culinary experience of the first water, for who can top Jacquiers? Of course, the Clarendon is unexceptional so far as a public hotel goes. Just the same, I must insist that you allow me to put you up here in Berkeley Square."

"You are very kind, Your Grace. I do appreciate the offer, but—"

"My dear, I beg you not to refuse. What with both sons married and no daughters to bear me company, I am reduced to rattling around in this enormous barn. It gets lonely, Jenny. Please say you'll join me."

Jenny gave a soft chuckle. "Now that you've so neatly backed me into a corner, what else can I say, but yes?"

"Splendid. Finish your tea while I ring for a carriage. I shall send a footman along to see to your luggage once your maid has repacked your things." The duchess gazed at Jenny suspiciously. "Your abigail did accompany you to London, did she not?"

"She did. However, she caught cold on our journey and I ordered her to spend the day in bed."

"In that case, I'll send one of the upstairs

maids to pack your trunk. As you see, I am bound and determined to establish you under my roof before nightfall."

Jenny stood and drew on her gloves. "You are very kind, Duchess. At what hour do we dine?"

"Eight sharp, but pray join me for a glass of sherry in the main drawing room around seven-thirty."

"Yes, I shall. And now I must fly."

"My dear Jenny, it is beyond wonderful to have you under my wing once again. First thing tomorrow morning we must drive up to Bloomsbury."

"Bloomsbury, ma'am?"

"Yes, to Mrs. Bell's establishment in Upper King Street. I feel certain you are dying to meet her after poring over the copperplates of the gowns she designs that appear monthly in *La Belle Assemblée*. Besides, she always has ready-made garments on hand that will serve in a pinch. And the bonnets she fashions are every bit as clever as her gowns. Any lady who crosses that portal can be outfitted from the skin out—all within the confines of a single roof. So much more convenient than wandering from shop to shop. Do you not agree?"

"But of course."

Jenny smiled to herself. Maybelle was incorrigible. And, as much as she loved the duchess, there was no denying Her Grace did not easily take no for an answer. Thus, even though she'd taken great pains to explain her true purpose in coming to London, Jenny knew Her Grace would badger her until she consented to attend at least some *tonnish* affairs.

No wonder she'd been so hesitant to call on the duchess, Jenny mused. Had she stopped to think, she might have guessed how things would progress from the moment she lifted the knocker. Certainly such an underlying suspicion would account for her insistence that the jarvey keep circling Berkeley Square instead of setting her down at once in front of Her Grace's town house.

Jenny chuckled, her spirits buoyant. Yes, Maybelle was incorrigible, but since she was here in London, it wouldn't hurt to acquire a little Town bronze, would it?

Thirteen

One more day and he'd reach the hunting box, Andrew thought as he approached the outskirts of Oakham. And he certainly would be glad to sleep in his own bed after four days on the road. Of course, he could have reached his destination sooner had he elected to travel post-chaise. But he'd wanted to give the new gig, custom designed by Tilbury, a trial run.

An hour later he pulled into the courtyard of the Fox and Hounds and surrendered his equipage to an ostler. Inside the inn, he commanded a simple meal of bread, cheese, and ale. When the taproom began to fill with local patrons, Andrew did not linger. Up in his room, he fell asleep the instant his head touched the pillow.

The next morning he heard the cock crow as he dressed. After a skimpy breakfast, he paid his shot and set off on the final leg of his journey. The road he traveled wound through gently rolling foothills adorned with newly minted grass dotted with buttercups and pink harrow. The air reverberated with the song of the meadowlark. And once the sun grew warm enough to melt the

morning dew, Andrew felt the air become the
perfect temperature. Nonetheless, his enthusiasm
for the bucolic beauty of the countryside had begun to wane by the time he sighted the hunting
box.

When he halted outside the front entrance, he
was startled by an unexpected welling of emotion
as poignant memories of the sweet innocent he'd
wed swamped his senses. Andrew regarded the
lodge with fresh eyes. This was where he and
Jenny had spent their honeymoon.

Shaken by the depth of his emotional response,
Andrew ruthlessly forced his thoughts down another, hopefully less turbulent, channel. Soon now,
he'd be reunited with his son. To be sure, Alexander would consider him an intruder—at least until they'd gotten to know each other better.

There was also Sandor's mother to consider.
He didn't want to step on her toes if he could
help it. Andrew's face softened as he recalled
Jenny's sweetness of temperament. Other memory
fragments surfaced. Some painful; some not. He
winced as he recalled the forlorn expression on
his wife's face when told he was leaving. The
wounded look in her eyes still haunted him, despite the passage of time.

Bloody hell! What a callous bastard he'd been.
At least now he was older and no longer quite
so enamored with his own consequence. As a
young cub, the world of diplomacy had glittered
and sparkled, but lately Andrew had begun to
wonder if what he'd perceived as gold had actu-

ally been dross. For certain, he was disgusted with the petty squabbling amongst England's allies that had flared up the past winter in Frankfurt and, which he understood from current dispatches, had continued on into the spring at the Congress of Vienna.

His father's death obliged him to quit the diplomatic service. He'd always known a time would come when he must. But, much to his surprise, when that day actually dawned, he'd found he had no regrets. On the contrary, he looked forward to assuming the responsibilities that went hand and hand with the title he'd inherited. Best of all, since he intended to lead a simpler life than before, Jenny could have a place in it. For he no longer cared to cut a dash—either in society or in diplomatic circles.

Like his father before him, Andrew meant to make Halpern Abbey his principal residence. Living quietly in the country, Jenny's social lacks would be far outweighed by her sunny disposition. Thus, as soon as the dust stirred up by his unheralded return settled, he planned to transport wife and son to the Abbey where the three of them could make a fresh start as a family.

He frowned. Time after time he'd begun a letter to Jenny informing her he'd changed his mind and wanted to try and make a go of their marriage. Time after time he'd ended up dissatisfied with what he wrote. Finally he'd decided it would be better to talk to her in person.

High overhead the raucous protest of a careening hawk grated on his eardrums. Shading his eyes with one hand, he peered up at the noisy scavenger whose wingspread temporarily blotted out the sun.

Andrew shuddered. *Someone had walked on his grave!* An instant later, the bright sunshine returned, assuaging the debilitating chill. Forehead furrowed, he watched the hawk merge with the horizon. Andrew considered himself to be the most pragmatic of men. He did not believe in ghosts or the supernatural. Yet he sensed something eerie inherent in the stillness as he peered with growing trepidation at the hunting box. His spirits plummeted. The place looked deserted. Had Jenny let the staff go? Since his father passed away six months ago, she could be in dire straits. Perhaps she'd been forced to dismiss all the servants.

Damnation! Furious with himself for not anticipating the bind Jenny might be in as a consequence of his delayed return to English soil, he gave the horse in harness the office to start.

As the gig approached the stables, Andrew continued to mentally chastise himself. He ought to have put his foot down when the news of his father's death had finally caught up to him in Frankfurt last December. He ought not have let Castlereagh persuade him to delay his departure. God knows what hardships Jenny had endured as a result of his tardiness.

As the gig drew flush with the stable door, a

young straw-headed lad materialized. Andrew climbed down and handed him the reins.

"G'day ta ya, m'lord."

"Hello, Will. How fare my wife and son?"

"I don't ken, m'lord," the boy said, looking puzzled.

"What do you mean you don't understand? I asked you a simple question. Where's my wife?" Andrew asked tightly, feeling short of breath.

"Gone, sar."

"Gone? Gone where? And what of my heir?"

"He be gone, too."

A black cloud of despair swirled about Andrew. Frustrated beyond bearing, he seized the front of the boy's shirt and gave him a vigorous shake. "Tell me the truth. Are they dead?"

"Oh no, sar. Yer family be well else we'd 'ave 'ad word."

Andrew took a firmer grip on the boy's shirt and raised the lad high enough for his feet to dangle. "Damn your eyes! You misled me. You deserve a sound thrashing."

Will snorted. "Fer wot? I be doin' me best to answer yer Tom Fool questions."

Andrew had to admire the boy's bravado, for he'd glimpsed raw fear in his eyes. Suddenly the urge to hit something or someone seemed unworthy. Ashamed of himself for playing the bully, he lowered the stableboy's feet to the ground and let go of his shirt.

"Sorry, lad. Blasted temper got the best of me.

I'm terribly worried about my family. I gather they no longer live on the premises?"

"Right, sar. They rid off nigh on two years ago."

The lad's revelation affected Andrew like a punch in the gut. "Two years?" he shouted, then, pressing his lips into a thin line, said in a quieter voice, "Two *years?*"

He halted the boy as Will, bridle in hand, started to move toward the stable. Andrew cast him a reassuring smile. "Don't be scared. All I want is information. For instance, do you have any idea why they left? Or where they went?"

"No, sar. But seeing as they went off with the old marquess, my guess be he took them to the Abbey."

Will's theory made sense. Andrew dug into a pocket and extracted a guinea which he tossed to the stableboy. "There you go, lad. Something for your trouble."

Will bit into the coin. Satisfied it was genuine, the grinning boy tugged on a forelock.

"See to my rig," Andrew ordered gruffly.

The scent of newly baked bread made his mouth water the instant Andrew set foot inside the kitchen. Despite the informal setting, Will's parents accorded him all the deference to which he was entitled, now that he'd stepped into his father's shoes.

Yet an hour later, Andrew was just as baffled as he'd been before he'd quizzed the caretaker. To be sure, he now knew it had been his father who'd paid off all the servants before he'd borne Jenny and Sandor off in his travel coach. Presumably he'd taken them to live with him at Halpern Abbey. But Andrew still had no idea what had prompted his father to meddle, and it troubled him.

However, close questioning of the caretaker's wife did reveal that Jenny had fallen gravely ill two months before she'd quit the hunting box. Fortunately for her, the same doctor who'd attended her during her confinement had managed to pull her through.

Andrew struck his forehead with his open palm. Why, of course! If nothing else, Dr. Ellers could furnish him with the particulars of Jenny's illness. He drained his coffee cup and made for the stable, where he ordered Will to hitch up the gig.

He spent the entire morning trailing the local sawbones as he made his rounds, several times missing his quarry by only a few minutes. Andrew finally caught up with the elusive doctor when he returned to the modest bungalow he regarded as home.

The interview did not progress as smoothly as Andrew could have wished. Frankly, Dr. Eller's constraint puzzled him, since their relationship had been cordial during the eighteen months Andrew had cohabited with Jenny. At that time, Ellers had struck him as a kindly practitioner whose frank open manner made him easy to confide in. But either Andrew's memory had played him false or Dr. Ellers had adopted a new personality. Whatever the reason, the warm compassionate man Andrew remembered was gone, and in his place stood a man whose cool reserve appeared virtually impenetrable.

Despite this formidable obstacle, the bare bones of a tale gradually surfaced. Weakened by childbirth, Jenny had almost died of diphtheria. According to Dr. Ellers, Andrew's father had arrived at the lodge shortly before the crisis point, and once Jenny was strong enough to be moved, the marquess had borne her and the children off.

"Children? You mean child, do you not?" asked Andrew with a superior smile.

Dr. Ellers glared at him coldly. "My lord, I do not regard your convenient memory lapse as a joking matter."

Andrew literally saw red. He'd taken all the abuse he'd intended to. "How dare you presume to judge me, sir?"

"Any man who callously neglects a wife who's borne him three sons is beneath contempt."

"Three sons? Are you saying Jenny played me false?" Andrew snarled.

"Why, you unspeakable blackguard! For your information, the new Lady Buxton gave birth to twin sons seven months after you heartlessly deserted her."

"Twins?"

Dr. Ellers nodded. "Aubrey and Alistair, born April 17, 1812."

"I'm the father of twins?" Initial awe gave way to indignation. "Why wasn't I told?"

The doctor regarded him sourly. "Lady Buxton wrote to you a month after their birth. Do you actually have the gall to claim you never received her letter?"

"But it's the truth! I didn't," Andrew shouted.

"So you claim, my lord, so you claim. Excuse me, I've patients waiting in the dispensary."

That night, Andrew could not sleep. Twins? The idea itself was mind-boggling. Poor Jenny. His cavalier assumption that she'd be perfectly all right living here at the hunting box now struck him as ludicrous. Whenever he stopped to consider the hardships she'd suffered thanks to his indifference, he was tempted to blow out his brains with one of his father's dueling pistols.

His mouth twisted in a sardonic grin. The fact that the prized set had never been kept on the premises tended to take the teeth out his bombastic posturing. Besides, he had no business contemplating suicide—not even fleetingly. Too many people depended upon him now that he'd assumed his father's title.

However, his principal concern was Jenny. True, he'd treated her abominably in the past. However, in the future he meant to make amends. But first, he had to find her. More than likely he'd discover her comfortably ensconced at the Abbey. Provided that's where she went, of course. But the odds favored it. After all, where else could she go? He'd soon know for certain if she were there. At first light, he'd set out for Devon.

A sennight later found Andrew pacing the anteroom of Silas Minton's office at 22 Chancery Lane. Dark circles ringed eyes that mirrored his desperation. Suffice to say he had not found Jenny at Halpern Abbey. And to make matters worse, the entire staff had clammed up on him.

Why, even the housekeeper, who'd known him since he'd been christened, had refused to open her budget. And since she and Birdie Pamphrey were sisters, she'd been his best bet. Under such trying circumstances, Andrew had learned precious little. Even more frustrating, the tidbits he'd managed to glean didn't make much sense.

Nonetheless, since he appeared to have nothing better to do than pace the floor, he might as well review what he knew in the hope that he might stumble upon something he'd overlooked that might prove useful. First of all, none of his sons had ever set foot inside the Abbey. True, the nursery had been scrubbed from top to bottom in anticipation of them spending the Christmas holidays there, but unfortunately their grandfather had died in early November.

As for Jenny, the only time she'd crossed the Abbey threshold was shortly before Andrew's father died. She'd stayed until after the services and then left, bound God knew where. These gleanings were the sum total of what he'd learned, because the servants had closed ranks against him.

Andrew halted his pacing to peer out a dirt-streaked window that overlooked the London's bustling business district. In all candor, he could not deny that he richly deserved everyone's censure. The problem was the servants' attitude made it devilishly difficult to find Jenny. With each passing day, he grew more frantic. He had to find her. How else could he make amends? And how could he be a father to his three sons if he didn't even know where they were?

Andrew was just beginning to wonder how much longer Minton intended to keep him cooling his heels when the connecting door between the anteroom and inner office swung open and Silas Minton's shrunken, bent figure sidled through the open doorway, bowing and scraping.

"My lord, I regret I was off on an errand when you arrived. Rest assured, I am honored that you chose to grace my humble office, even though I would have been most happy to call at your town house."

"It's in Holland covers. And since time is of the essence, I decided to venture into the city."

"I see. Please step into my office."

Once he did, he found himself at the mercy of the fawning solicitor, who'd handled his business affairs since he'd reached his majority. Andrew impatiently brushed aside a veritable stream of effusive compliments.

"Spare me my blushes, Minton. To my utter astonishment, I learned from the doctor in Leicestershire that in addition to my heir, my wife bore me twins two years ago this month. Are you aware of this?"

"Why certainly."

"The devil you say!"

Silas Minton regarded him searchingly. "Pardon my frankness, but is there any question that they are your get?"

The back of Andrew's neck burned, and he soon felt the spread of molten heat as the angry color climbed to the roots of his hair.

"Were you a gentleman, I'd call you out. What you imply is not only an insult to me but also to my wife."

"I meant no offense," Minton whined. "I was merely trying to ascertain why you are overset. Before you went abroad, you made it very clear that once your wife had produced an heir, you had no further interest in her."

Had he actually told Minton that? He suspected he had. Andrew sighed. He had much to answer for. "Never mind what I said. Tell me, did Jenny send me a letter apprising me of their birth?"

"Why, yes, she did."

"Devil take you, sir. Why didn't you forward it to me?"

Minton looked much put upon. "But I did forward it, sir."

"Really? Devilishy odd that I never received it, don't you agree?"

"My lord, why all the fuss over a letter? When you placed me in sole charge of Lady Buxton's welfare, you stressed that you did not wish to be bothered with trivial details."

"What? Do you actually have the gall to tell me you consider the birth of twins a triviality?"

"Allow me to explain the circumstances. Accompanying her letter to you, your wife sent a cover letter addressed to me. It related the birth of the twins and requested that I direct the enclosed missive to you. Since you'd given me to understand you did not wish to be pestered by her, I did not deem her letter sufficiently important to go via diplomatic pouch. So instead, I sent it by regular post and increased her quarterly allowance by twenty-five pounds."

"Twenty-five pounds? Why such a paltry sum?"

"My lord, the twins were scare a month old. I saw no reason to encourage your wife to become a spendthrift. Had she applied to me later on, I was prepared to be a trifle more generous. However, she never wrote again."

"In light of your munificent increase in her allowance, no doubt she thought it would be a waste of postage," Andrew said in a voice dripping with sarcasm.

"My lord, you asked me to use my own judgment and not bother you unnecessarily. I hardly think it fair for you to attack me for following your instructions to the letter."

"Yes, yes, I'm well aware that I must bear the brunt of the blame. But how was I to know you could be so heartless? Tell me, sir, did it never occur to you that having three sons instead of one to feed and clothe might severely tax such a modest stipend?"

"I thought I'd already made it clear that had she again applied for an increase, I probably would have granted her additional funds, notwithstanding the fact that, several months after the twins' birth, your father wrote instructing me to send her quarterly allowance to the business manager he'd engaged to handle your wife's affairs, instead of to the bank in Melton as I'd done formerly."

"So my father chose to stick his nose in my private affairs. I cannot pretend to like it. However, since I was abroad, I suppose I must be grateful that he took an interest in my wife's welfare."

"Just so, my lord. Which brings us to the reason I did not worry overmuch as to how the then Lady Temple was managing to pay her bills."

"You thought my father was supplementing her income?"

"Your assumption is correct, my lord."

There was a short pause before Andrew worked up the nerve to ask, "The cover letter Jenny wrote to you. Do you still have it?"

"Why yes. Would you like to see it?"

"Please."

Minton rang for a clerk who returned minutes later with the requested folder. The solicitor rifled through the papers inside until he found Jenny's cover letter, which he handed to Andrew.

Andrew's throat clogged and his eyes misted as

he gazed at Jenny's elegant script. How hurt she must have been when she'd received no reply. How she must have despised his indifference.

He shifted his gaze to Silas Minton and asked, "Mind if I keep it?"

Minton regarded Andrew as if he had two heads, then shrugged. "Not at all, my lord. You're welcome to it."

A wave of tenderness for his long-suffering wife swept through Andrew as he slipped her letter into an inside pocket of his waistcoat. No doubt the twins were two-year-old terrors who, along with their elder brother, would be quite a handful for any young mother to manage. His sons needed the firm hand of a father to insure they toed the line.

It was imperative that he find Jenny. And the sooner the better. Because, even if his father had assisted her monetarily, he'd died six months ago. So how was she faring at present on the paltry sum his stingy man of business had deemed sufficient?

Andrew managed a painful swallow despite the lump in his throat. What if he found her and his sons on the brink of starvation? The unwelcome thought filled him with horror.

Jenny would never forgive him. Nor did he deserve to be forgiven. Come to that, he'd never forgive himself.

He glared at Minton with such ferocity that the poor solicitor flinched. Choking back his anger, Andrew obtained the direction of Jenny's man of

business, then quit the premises before he gave
in to temptation and actually throttled the trembling old miser.

Fourteen

Andrew was glad he'd decided to come. The day he'd just put in had been pure hell from start to finish, and he badly needed a diversion to wash away the bad taste it had left in his mouth.

The truth was he was used to achieving his goals with minimal effort. But not this time. Never before had he felt such frustration. Never before had he seen the specter of failure staring him in the face. Never before had he suffered such a crushing defeat.

Andrew sighed. Discovering Jenny's whereabouts was beginning to seem like a quest for the Holy Grail. His lips twisted in a cynical smile. He'd always prided himself on his ability to maintain his perspective. But for the first time in his entire life, he sensed that if he weren't careful, his need to find Jenny just might drive him to Bedlam.

Thus, Piers's invitation to accompany him to this evening's performance of *The Country Girl* had seemed like a lifeline.

Once inside the theater, he'd realized that passive attendance alone would not answer. To achieve a respite from his present problems, he must shake off his doldrums and immerse himself in every nuance of tonight's performance—both onstage and off.

Determined to soak up atmosphere, he let his mind drift. Animated conversations emanating from the one-shilling gallery and from the three tiers of private boxes housing members of the nobility mingled with blunt exchanges between tradesmen conducted in the balcony directly overhead, as well as those taking place in a second balcony, so high up it flirted with the theater's dome-shaped ceiling.

Andrew shook his head in wonder. It stood to reason that the intertwining of voices, running the gamut from cultured upper-class English to Cockney, should result in a modern-day version of the Tower of Babel. Instead, the feisty blend of voices from all walks of life had manifested itself in a low-keyed buzz not at all unpleasant to the ear.

"Botheration!"

Curiosity piqued, Andrew peered at his companion. "What vexes you, Piers?"

"Spotted my nephew in the gallery."

"So?"

"Promised my sister to keep an eye on him. Silly young cub constantly lands in the suds." Shelwyn shook his blond head.

"Just what is he doing that has you mad as a buck?"

"Roger's making a cake of himself ogling the ladies. Idiot makes no distinction between Cyprians and highborn beauties."

"How very democratic of Moreton, to be sure," Andrew observed, tongue in cheek.

"Go straight to the devil, Andy!"

"Now, Piers, no need to snap my head off. Show some sense. Roger respects you. Why not encourage him to express his admiration more discreetly?"

Shelwyn slapped Andrew on the back. "By God, you're right. I'll stage a man-to-man talk. If I employ a little tact, I think he'll listen."

Andrew scanned the gallery until he found the young man under discussion. "Take a gander at Moreton's cronies, old stick. Unless my eyes deceive me, they're every bit as smitten as your feckless nephew. Shall we see if we can discover the identity of the charmer who's enslaved every man Jack in the gallery?"

Shelwyn stiffened. "You forget I'm a married man."

Andrew arched an eyebrow. "So am I, come to that. Courage, chum. You may be married, but you're not dead yet."

Shelwyn gave a wry chuckle. "I will be if Eleanor catches me ogling another female."

Andrew gave a roar of laughter. It was good to know that he hadn't forgotten how, though God knows he hadn't done much laughing lately.

Little wonder. Today he'd called on Jenny's man of business fully confident of obtaining her direction. After all, what businessman in his right mind would dare deny a husband access to his own wife? Especially since in the eyes of the law, Jenny was his property to deal with as he saw fit.

Instead, to his amazement, the man had categorically denied that either Viscountess Temple or the new Marchioness of Buxton was, or had ever been, a client.

Even now, hours later, Andrew vividly recalled how desperate he'd felt when his promising lead had fizzled. He still remembered the decidedly queasy sensation in the pit of his stomach when he'd realized that he had no idea whether or not the accountant was telling him a baldfaced lie or the truth. All he knew for certain was that he must find Jenny. Yet he hadn't the foggiest notion of where else to look. Or what to do next. Even worse, without her direction, he was at a standstill. So frustrating!

Fortunately for his sanity, before despair could trigger a decline, Piers had dropped by his town house to drag him off to Covent Garden. So here he sat, Andrew mused, doing his level best to soothe his friend's ruffled feathers. Interestingly enough, by drawing a bead between the young bucks restlessly milling in the gallery and the reserved box on the opposite wall, he managed to pinpoint the location of the siren responsible for capturing the eye of every lovesick swain manning the gallery.

Instantaneously Andrew felt his pulse quicken as he studied the lovely young woman seated be-

side the Dowager Duchess of Dillon. Her hair wa
the color of dark honey; her skin put him i
mind of magnolias. Wanting to reach out an
touch her cheek, he bitterly regretted they wer
separated by the width of the theater.

Andrew's eyes narrowed. He gave a harsh bar
of laughter. Magnolias indeed! He had no busi
ness mooning over the beautiful creature oppo
site. He must not lose sight of his purpose o
coming to London. First thing tomorrow morn
ing, he'd hie to Bow Street and hire a runner t
help him find Jenny.

Across the way, the Dowager Duchess of Dillon
turned to her companion. "My dear, have yo
noticed how many noblemen are discreetly oglin
you?"

"Stuff!" Jenny scoffed. "Why on earth woul
the *ton* be interested in homely Mrs. Shaw?"

"Homely? Whenever did you get such a crack
brained idea?"

"Give over, Your Grace. I was born homely."

The sad wistfulness in Jenny's eyes, couple
with the break in her voice, swept the incredulou
scowl off the duchess's countenance. "Lord, gran
me patience! You are not homely. On the con
trary, you are beautiful."

"Ma'am, there's no need to lie."

Maybelle stared at her prodigy nonplussed
Was it possible that Jenny did not realize she wa
stunningly beautiful? Or that, should she so de
sire, all she need do was to show some sign tha

she welcomed their attentions to have the entire male population of Mayfair at her feet?

"Saints preserve us!" the duchess said impatiently. "I'm tempted to shake some sense into you. I venture to say you are one of the most beautiful ladies in the entire theater."

Disconcerted, Jenny nibbled on her lower lip. Perhaps she was not quite as homely as she used to be, back when she'd been stuck with an unruly crop of downy yellow fluff. Indeed, she'd be the first to admit that her present thick mane of dark honey hair was a vast improvement. But to call her a beauty was doing things up too brown.

The duchess laughed. "You don't believe you are beautiful, do you?"

"Of course not."

"Well, since you won't trust my judgment, do yourself a favor. Take a good look around the theater. I'm curious to see if you can deny the evidence of your own eyes."

Rising to the challenge, Jenny hazarded a cautious peek at the gallery. Despite Maybelle's assertion, she was rather taken aback to discover a handsome young dandy peering up at her through a quizzing glass. She hastily shifted her gaze, but each and every place she looked seemed occupied by a brazen male who apparently hadn't been taught at his mother's knee that it was rude to stare.

"Fiddlestick!"

"Just so," said the duchess.

Jenny shook her head vigorously. "I'll grant

you all the world and his brother are staring. But not at me, I promise you."

"Humbug! I've attended countless performances without ever becoming the cynosure of all eyes."

"Then something else must have caught their eye."

Maybelle lifted an eyebrow. "What, pray tell?"

"I don't know, ma'am. But something has . . ." Jenny's knitted brow cleared. "But of course! It's my new Platoff cap. It's all the rage."

"Fustian! The ladies are not staring, the gentlemen are." The duchess's gaze softened. "Face facts, my dear. It's neither your cap nor your new gown that sparks their interest. It's you, Jenny. Furthermore, it's not just the gallery that's interested in the unknown beauty seated beside me. You've also captured the hearts of the noblemen in private boxes."

Jenny darted a wary glance across the way. Mercy! The duchess was right. Every male in the theater appeared to be staring at her. The awesome thought unnerved her. She wrung her hands.

"Truly, ma'am, it cannot be me they are mooning over. I'm not beautiful; I'm homely."

The Duchess of Dillon gave a frustrated sigh. What she wouldn't give to convince Jenny that she was a diamond of the first water. "Child, your excessive modesty grows tiresome. The warning bell has sounded. Fix your gaze upon the stage. The curtain is about to rise."

Jenny was only too happy to oblige. Engrossed

in the play, she soon forgot all else and simply enjoyed the performance. As a consequence, at the conclusion of the first act, her sides ached from laughing so hard.

Once the houselights came up, she looked askance at the duchess. "Mrs. Jordan is superb, don't you agree?"

Maybelle issued a sly grin. "Indeed, her comedic timing has no rival. However, while she plays the innocent ingenue to perfection, Mrs. Jordan is certainly no innocent in her private life—not with all those little FitzClarences eating her out of house and home."

"FitzClarences, ma'am?"

The duchess nodded. "Mrs. Jordan is the Duke of Clarence's mistress. Talented actress or no, one can only be sorry for the misguided creature."

"Because her children are illegitimate?" asked Jenny.

"That's not the half of it. You see, Clarence does not fully support all those pledges of her devotion; she does. Time and again she is forced out of retirement to make ends meet. Not that it isn't a rare treat for the public, of course."

Watching Maybelle raise her opera glasses and peer through them, Jenny felt torn between amusement and disapproval. "How disobliging of the Royal Duke. Is there no way to prod him into being more generous?"

"If there is, Mrs. Jordan has yet to discover it."

The duchess held out the opera glasses and smiled at Jenny. "Brummell's holding court across the way. You are welcome to borrow these if you want a peek."

"Really? I'd like to try them out."

Achieving proper focus took patience, but once she'd mastered the skill, she espied the famed dandy. Even at a distance, it was not difficult to see why he'd been dubbed the harbinger of male fashion. Jenny scanned several other theater parties. However, her perusal came to a jarring halt once she focused upon the box directly opposite. Her shocked gasp drew the duchess's attention.

"My dear, what's amiss?"

The light of battle in her eyes, Jenny thrust the opera glasses toward Maybelle. "Take them back. I've seen my fill."

Clearly puzzled, the duchess took possession of the glasses. "Child, you're white as a sheet. Have you seen a ghost?"

"No, not a ghost. What I see is my husband. Even more aggravating, a beautiful woman is hanging on his sleeve. I'd like to scratch her eyes out!"

"Jenny! Do curb your temper." The duchess peered through the lens. "Take heart, child. At least he's not alone with her. Lord Shelwyn is with him."

As if the presence of his crony would make the slightest difference to a confirmed rake, Jenny silently fumed as Maybelle lowered the opera glasses and beamed her a smile.

"I'd forgotten what a handsome devil your husband is."

"Never mind his looks," Jenny snapped. "Who is she?"

The duchess sighed. "Since you insist, she is Sara, the recently divorced Marchioness of Quinlan."

Jenny visibly paled. She almost wished her father-in-law hadn't confided in her last autumn. At times such as this, she suspected that ignorance was truly bliss.

"Your Grace, perhaps we should leave."

"If you truly wish to, we shall. But first, I beg leave to tell you it goes against the grain to retreat in the face of that shameless hussy."

"A telling point, ma'am. However, Andrew may cut up stiff if he discovers me traveling in such elevated circles. You see, he has absolutely no faith that I could ever be a credit to him in society."

The duchess snorted. "All the more reason to prove him wrong. Besides, I thought you were looking forward to seeing the second act."

"Oh, I was. Especially as I shall probably never get another chance to see Mrs. Jordan play Peggy. But Andrew might lose his temper if he spots me."

"What if he does? He's not likely to strike you in public, is he?"

Jenny looked horrified. "Certainly not. Nor in private either. Andrew does not strike women."

"Excellent. At least there's something that can be said in his favor," Maybelle observed wryly. "Jenny, I shall leave it up to you whether we stay or go. But, in your shoes, I would never give ground."

The gaslights gradually dimmed. Jenny knew she must make a decision. Preferably before the entire audience was plunged into darkness, rendering dignified retreat awkward. Chin set at a belligerent angle, she said, "Not only do I refuse to show the white feather, I don't intend to allow *anyone* to spoil my evening."

True to her word, Jenny soon became caught up in the light-hearted farce featuring Mrs. Jordan, whose innate naiveté made her such a pleasure to watch. Thus, when the houselights came up at the end of the second act, Jenny was quick to join in the enthusiastic applause.

Soon after it died and the houselights brightened, the rustle of the red silk curtain being shuttled aside drew both ladies' attention. Craning her neck, the duchess smiled at Roger Moreton as he moved forward to make room for several of his cronies. When he returned her smile, Maybelle decided he was a cocky young sprig. When he made her an elegant leg, she decided there was no real harm in him. When he straightened and she saw his flushed face, she exclaimed, "Gracious me! You must have ran the entire way in order to get here so fast."

"Of course I did. How else could I steal the march on your beautiful companion's other admirers?"

"How enterprising of you to be sure!" Still chuckling at his audacity, the duchess turned to

enny. "My dear, allow me to present Mr. More-
on. Moreton, Mrs. Shaw."

Andrew entered the duchess's box close on the
heels of the anxious Lord Shelwyn, whose plan
to intercept his nephew en route had failed by a
whisker and who was now down in the dumps as
a result. Andrew wished Piers were in a better
mood, but since he could think of no way to
lighten it, he turned his attention to placating the
dragon guarding the beauty.

He and the outspoken dowager duchess were
not close acquaintances. Nonetheless, what little
he'd seen of her, he'd liked. In his opinion, the
lovely young woman, whom Her Grace introduced
to one and all as Mrs. Shaw, could count herself
lucky to have acquired such a formidable sponsor.

However, despite his worldly cynicism, when it
became his turn to strut like a peacock before
the Incomparable, Andrew found himself help-
lessly enchanted by her furtive peek at his face
before she swiftly lowered her lashes.

Look up. Please look up, he silently pleaded, even
as he wondered why it seemed so important to
him that their eyes meet. Miraculously, as if she'd
divined his thoughts, the shy beauty peered up
at him. The instant their eyes locked, Andrew lost
himself in her golden gaze.

Mesmerized, Andrew forgot all about Pier's
problems. He forgot all about his search for
Jenny. Hell, he even forgot his own name. None
of the other people occupying the box existed.
Only the two of them did.

He'd guessed right about the texture of her skin. Now close enough, he dared not reach out and touch it—though God knew he wanted to with an intensity that almost unmanned him. Her dark honey tresses had been swept up toward her crown, then allowed to tumble in artless curls that he found charming. However, it was the flicker of naked yearning on her face that captivated him.

Ah, my golden-eyed beauty, we meet too late to be come soul mates. Patience, my darling. Another place. Another time. I'll be free to love you, I promise.

Ever afterward, Andrew was unable to say who broke eye contact first. One minute their gazes interlocked. The next, he felt as if he'd been cut adrift. He broke out in a cold sweat as he became keenly aware of the stagnant air and cramped quarters. No great surprise, since the beauty's admirers were crammed like sardines into the relatively small box. Forced to take shallow breaths and fighting an almost overwhelming fear of suffocation, he took a backward step, his retreat allowing a fresh surge of gallants access to the beautiful Mrs. Shaw.

Craving a breath of fresh air, Andrew bolted. He was halfway back to the box Piers had rented before he realized that Shelwyn had kept pace with him. Andrew experienced a twinge of guilt. Once he'd come face to face to the Incomparable, nothing and no one else had existed except the beauty who'd trapped him in her web.

As the golden vision continued to shimmer in

is mind's eye, Andrew wondered if Mrs. Shaw
were a witch. If true, it would account for his
falling under her spell. Her eyes weren't actually
golden; they were . . . ? Andrew shrugged.
Whatever their color, they were quite lovely.

The Duchess of Dillon's mobile features registered equal parts amusement and annoyance in
the face of the Marquess of Buxton's abrupt retreat. Particularly in light of the warm regard
he'd seen in his eyes when she'd slyly introduced
him to his own wife.

The warning bell signaled a mass exodus from
the dowager duchess's box. It brought a heartfelt
sigh of relief from Jenny, which in turn caused
Maybelle to glance at her prodigy. "My dear, are
you all right?"

"At the moment, I'm too overwhelmed to tell."

The duchess laughed. "So many gentlemen at
your feet has to be flattering."

Jenny grinned. "I must admit to be showered
with compliments felt very good at first. However,
I really don't think I'd enjoy playing goddess on
a pedestal on a permanent basis."

"Perhaps not. But the sincere regard of other
noblemen cannot help but raise your standing in
your husband's eyes."

Jenny's expression grew wistful. "I certainly
wish it. The sad truth is, Andrew didn't recognize
me."

"I received the same impression. Yet how can
that be?"

Jenny sighed. "To be fair to Andrew, assuming

he ever thinks of me at all, no doubt he envision
an earlier, homelier version."

"Incredible. Another thing I cannot under
stand is why he never blinked an eye when I in
troduced you as Mrs. Shaw."

Unspilt tears glistened in Jenny's eyes. "Clearl
either he's forgotten my maiden name or h
never bothered to learn it in the first place."

"Odious man!" exclaimed the duchess. "If you
ask me, 'tis high time he were taken down a peg."

Fifteen

Two days later, the Dowager Duchess of Dillon wept into Jenny's bedchamber. Spying the open trunk, she unfurled her fan and waved it back and forth with agitated vigor.

"I see you are nearly all packed."

Jenny sent a silent plea for forgiveness toward her obviously disgruntled hostess. "Your Grace, I'm sorry to disappoint you. I should never have made a rash promise to extend my visit."

Maybelle rolled her eyes. "Lord, grant me patience! How can you be so chicken-hearted as to leave the field open to that . . . that hussy?"

"What does it matter if I stay or go? The truth is an icicle in hell has a better chance of winning Andrew's regard than I do."

"Nonsense! If nothing else, 'tis plain your husband admires your beauty. I saw it in his eyes when I introduced you."

"Your Grace, you are allowing friendship to blind your perception. Granted, my looks have improved since he last set eyes on me, but one cannot make a silk purse out of a sow's ear."

" 'Tis you who have a blind spot, my dear. But

I don't propose to quibble. The point is Buxton perceives you as the beautiful Mrs. Shaw. All you need do is crook your finger and he'll fall at your feet. Don't you see? This is your chance to shine, Jenny. Don't waste it. Stay and fight."

Jenny bit the inside of her bottom lip so hard she tasted blood. "You will think me a coward, but I simply cannot bear to watch Lady Quinlan fawning over Andrew as she did yesterday afternoon in Hyde Park and a few nights ago at Covent Garden."

The duchess's gaze softened. "You still love him, do you not?"

"God help me, yes, I do."

"So I thought. I know his failure to recognize you rankles. Still, to bury yourself in Torquay solves nothing. Are you certain I cannot persuade you to stay?"

Jenny's eyes pleaded for understanding. "If Andrew truly wished to extricate himself from her clutches, he's perfectly capable of issuing the cut direct."

"Lady Quinlan is no longer received. Perhaps he cannot bring himself to be so heartless."

"All the more reason why I must not linger. Should my true identity become known, 'tis bound to revive the crim. con. case. Forgive me, but I feel I've already suffered enough indignities and will not willingly become fodder for the gossip mill."

"But, my dear, what about your book?"

"I called on Jasper Brownnell at his printshop two mornings ago and signed the contract."

"Did you indeed? I assume you've ironed out your differences?"

Jenny nodded. "The final stumbling block was the title. So we compromised. I get to keep my choice while Mr. Brownnell's preference becomes the subtitle. *Flora Domestica; or The Portable Flower Garden* is scheduled for publication in September."

"Excellent! Which reminds me, have I told you how proud I am of you, my dear?"

Jenny grinned. "Countless times."

Maybelle snapped her fan shut. "Since your resolve is firm, I shan't waste another breath coaxing you to stay. Which is not to say that I won't miss your company."

"And I yours."

"Quite right!"

Her Grace's parting smile did not quite hide her disappointment, and once she withdrew, Jenny sought a distraction to mitigate lingering twinges of guilt. The gown lying on her bed was the one she'd worn to Covent Garden. Was she doing the right thing? she wondered as she placed a layer of tissue paper over it, then folded its long, fitted sleeves across the bodice. The sleeves were trimmed from shoulder to cuff with row after row of delicate Mechlin lace, and truth be told, she'd coveted the evening dress from the instant she'd laid eyes upon it. However, when Mrs. Bell at *Magazine de Moules* quoted a sum far

above the amount she'd budgeted, she'd decided
the price was too steep.

A grave miscalculation on her part, Jenny now
conceded with a rueful smile as she placed the
pale lavender robe of the finest Indian muslin
along with an underdress of ecru satin—both garments swaddled in tissue—inside her trunk. For
Maybelle had insisted upon buying the dress for
her. Even in the face of Jenny's adamant refusal
to accept such an expensive gift, Her Grace had
remained obdurate. Eventually, her most telling
point, the gown's suitability for a young matron
in half mourning, had won the day. Thus, a triumphant dowager duchess had presented the evening dress to Jenny with the tactful suggestion
that she regard it as an early birthday present.
In the face of such generosity, Jenny had felt it
would be churlish to refuse. So she'd swallowed
her pride and graciously accepted the gown.

Andrew's dark blue eyes clouded. Nothing
seemed to go as planned. He'd had high hopes
when he'd engaged a Bow Street Runner to aid
in his search for Jenny. However, after a fortnight
in which the cocky red-vested runner turned up
nary a clue, he'd dismissed him. What Andrew
had found particularly demoralizing was the fact
that he hadn't the slightest idea where to turn
next. Yet concern for Jenny's welfare drove him.
He dare not stop searching. Because he knew
he'd get no rest, no peace, until he found her.

Deeply discouraged, he'd literally teetered on he brink of a crushing defeat until it finally lawned on him that his father must have sent his carriage to fetch Jenny to Halpern Abbey.

Exhilarated, Andrew's mind raced. *Why, of course!* he thought. *If anyone knew her present whereabouts, it was John Coachman.* Excitement vying with anticipation, Andrew tossed toiletries along with a clean shirt and a change of smalls into a valise, and quit London for Sticklepath.

Still, bad luck continued to dog him. Upon his arrival at Halpern Abbey four days later, he'd suffered yet another setback. Not only was John Coachman no longer in residence, prying his direction from the recalcitrant housekeeper had proved every bit as difficult as pulling hot chestnuts out of the fire. However, at long last, armed with the information that the coachman had retired to Plymouth, he'd traveled there by postchaise.

Thus now, inside the thatched-roof cottage with whitewashed walls, forced to confront his unwelcome visitor, the coachman grudgingly ordered his daughter to brew them a pot of tea, then glared at Andrew from watery blue eyes and warned, "Don't expect me to open me mummer until after I've drunk it neither."

Andrew's mouth twitched. The crusty old codger tickled his funnybone. Yet his countenance sobered once he'd had a chance to study the man's face. Indeed, his skin was the texture of shoe leather and boasted more crisscross lines than a roadmap—no doubt the result of thirty years spent on the box in all kinds of weather.

The old man's weather-beaten appearance didn't faze Andrew, but his stubborn stance did crossed arms resting upon a barrel chest and a lantern jaw thrusting belligerently. Andrew sighed. Prying Jenny's direction out of the ornery old coachman's tightly closed mouth was going to be harder than pulling teeth with a set of rusty pliers.

"Old Mother Hubbard went to the cupboard to get her poor dog a bone. But when she got there the—"

Jenny broke off reading to address the elder twin. "Dearest Aubrey, do stop trying to usurp your brother's place. You sat next to me last night. 'Tis Alistair's turn."

"But, Mama—"

"No buts, young man. Either settle down or be banished to the nursery."

Aubrey glowered at his twin as if he held his sibling personally responsible for the reprimand delivered by the mother they shared. Fortunately for all parties, Alistair remained blissfully ignorant of his brother's vengeful look, due to his rapt interest in the book on his mother's lap.

Small wonder, Jenny mused. First published in 1805, *The Comic Adventures of Old Mother Hubbard and Her Dog* had broken new ground by becoming the first English children's book to feature colored illustrations. A decade later, the book's watercolored pictures, hand-painted by children in their teens, and its nonsensical verses were still favored by enlightened parents and their offspring.

Alexander bestowed a wet kiss on Jenny's cheek. "Mama, I am so glad you came home."

Love poured out of Jenny as she gazed at her eldest son. The fact that Sandor had inherited both Andrew's beguiling smile and his unusual dark blue eyes caused a twinge of regret in regard to the estrangement between herself and the children's father.

"Are you glad to be home, too, Mama?"

"Of a certainty," she said, smiling gently.

Home. Indeed, it felt good to be here with her sons once more. Because despite all the diversions London had to offer, she'd sorely missed her children. A tiny frown disturbed her brow. Four years seemed a long time away, Jenny mused. Yet she suspected it would slip by all too fast. All she could do was to savor every minute spent with all three boys before they grew old enough for their father to take an interest in them. Assuming Andrew actually intended to take an active part in their lives, of course.

Her frown deepened. If nothing else, she supposed he would feel duty bound to display at least a modicum of paternal guidance—especially in Sandor's case, since he was his heir. As for the twins, despite the fact that so far all he'd displayed was total indifference, who could say what his attitude would be later on? All in all, it was probably just as well she'd decided to retire from the London scene before she succumbed to the temptation to comb Andrew's hair because of his casual assumption that the boys would flourish despite the lack of a father's influence in the formative years.

Her musings were broken by all three boys' impatient clamor that she finish the story. Indeed, she was thoroughly amused by the haughty annoyance she saw reflected in Sandor's dark blue eyes. It reminded her of Andrew in one of his autocratic moods. Whereas, unless her memory proved faulty, the twins' brown-green eyes were not only the same color as her scholarly father's, they held the same dreamy expression she'd seen all too often in his gaze.

Jenny offered up a silent prayer that they had not inherited their grandfather's reclusive tendencies as well. Bad enough that all three boys were towheads. Far worse, in her judgment, was the fact that they'd all inherited the fluffy, flyaway hair which had been the bane of her existence before diphtheria had rendered her temporarily bald.

She lifted the finger she'd used to mark her place. But even as she resumed reading aloud, she remembered to savor the moment. Because, in her opinion, nothing felt so good, so right as it did to be seated upon the faded chintz sofa surrounded by her three sons. Indeed, nothing compared to the clean sweet smell of their freshly bathed bodies huddled as close to her as they could manage. Nor did anything equal the rapt expression on each boy's face as the words she spoke created pictures in their minds. To Jenny, nothing equaled the closeness she felt at this moment as her three imps, who'd raced up and down the beach all day long, were now content to sit reasonably still while the woman who'd borne them read them a bedtime story. Truth to tell, Jenny likened the present sense of shared contentment to the closeness she'd felt during the months she'd carried them in her womb.

Jenny smiled to herself. Most definitely a moment to savor.

As expected, John Coachman had been as ornery as they come, forcing Andrew to call upon his considerable diplomatic skills to convince the crusty pensioner to loosen his tongue. But once he'd persuaded him to reveal Jenny's direction, Andrew's spirits had soared. In high glee, he'd insisted upon pressing on at once, serenely confident that since he now knew the name of the beach town, finding Jenny would be simple. Even when he'd arrived in Torquay late yesterday afternoon to discover the entire village shrouded in a heavy fog bank, his exuberant mood had held. Conceding that the weather was perfect for smugglers and not wishing to run afoul of the local "gentlemen," he'd reluctantly postponed his reunion with Jenny until the next day.

However, despite the fact that for the first time in weeks he'd slept like a baby, once again Andrew's plans went awry, chiefly because he'd never envisioned such a profusion of seaside cottages from which to pick. Thus, after a long, fruitless hike along the shoreline, Andrew decided that his present hit-or-miss method was not working and temporarily abandoned his search.

After all, he reasoned, only an addlewit went rushing off half-cocked. By rights, before quitting Plymouth, he ought to have pinned the coachman down as to precise location of the cottage. But since he had not, a fresh approach was necessary.

Inside a coffeehouse, tucked into an alley off the main thoroughfare, Andrew nursed a cup of coffee while mulling over his next move. A half-hour later, he tossed a few coins on the table and left the premises, armed with a list of local rental agents supplied by the proprietor.

In the expectation that Jenny had leased her cottage from one of the names on the list, Andrew spent the balance of the morning contacting each agent in turn. Unhappily, not one of the agents he spoke to would admit they'd ever heard of Lady Temple or Lord Buxton—much less had business dealings with either. Leaving yet another rental office, Andrew ground his teeth. The fact that his latest plan didn't seem to be working any better than his random search of the shoreline was a bitter pill to swallow.

By midday his frustration reached the boiling point. Grim-faced, he acknowledged if he didn't give vent to his seething temper, his head just might explode. He uttered a few pithy curses under his breath before trudging off to confront the last name on his list.

"Well, sar, far be it for me to contradict the gentry, but I'll tell ye straight out: if you be Lord Buxton, then I be a Dutchman!"

The rental agent's feisty rejoinder jolted Andrew from a fit of the dismals that had threatened to hamstring his progress. He smiled at the agent, who'd all but called him a liar. Wonder of wonders, he'd apparently stumbled onto the very fellow who could help him. Come to that, he could kick himself for not realizing beforehand that he ought to have focused his investigation on his father, who'd, more likely than not, signed the lease.

Mindful of the glimmer of suspicion in the agent's eye, Andrew treated him to his most disarming smile. "My father was the seventh Marquess of Buxton. I inherited the title when he passed away last November. I collect you had business dealings with him."

"I 'ad that 'oner, sar . . . er, yer lordship."

"I believe he leased a seaside cottage." Andrew's raised eyebrow fell just short of converting a statement into a question.

"Aye, sar, fer the sake of 'is daughter-in-law's 'ealth."

The agent's response played hell with Andrew's

shaky sanguinity, but he managed a cool response. "So I've been told. At present, I am anxious to rejoin my wife and family, and require the exact location of the cottage my father leased for them, if you would be so kind?"

"Most 'appy to be of service, yer lordship."

Assured that the house he sought lay within easy walking distance, Andrew set off on foot. Ten minutes later, he paused before a thatched cottage to drink in the subtle fragrance of climbing roses that partially obscured thick mud-plaster walls boasting a fresh coat of whitewash.

Andrew had to smile. The bucolic setting suited Jenny. Unsophisticated, even homely, but nonetheless restful and unpretentious.

Sixteen

Jenny sat cross-legged on a bed of fine white sand, her slim, straight back facing the cottage. A bright red ribbon secured her hair at her crown, its streamers flapping in the breeze. Her cotton shift had clearly seen better days, but here at the seashore she need not be fashionable. She could dress for comfort.

Sunrays danced atop the surface of the water to create a diamondlike dazzle that temporarily blinded her. Several rapid blinks later, she spotted her eldest son lugging a pail of water, its contents sloshing over the edges. Sandor was biting his tongue, something he did whenever he tackled a difficult task. Watching him struggle, her heart did a crazy flip-flop.

Focusing on the horizon, she drew a deep breath. She reveled in the sharp, salty tang of sea air blowing landward from choppy Channel waters just beyond the stone breakwater, constructed to create a safe harbor for sailors, fishermen, and small rambunctious boys, who liked to paddle about in the shallows and to build sandcastles. And in Sandor's case, Jenny thought with an indulgent smile, to scramble over the boulders before she had put a stop to it.

Overhead, gulls cawed and careened. Jenny decided it was time to set loose the last vestiges of resentment she'd carried with her all the way from London like excess baggage. For how could she possibly feel sorry for herself when blessed with three lively sons to brighten her days?

Huffing and puffing, Sandor set down the pail he'd been lugging and dropped to his knees.

"Is this enough water, or should I make another trip?"

Jenny glanced at the half-empty pail and bit back a bubble of laughter. "It will do for a nonce. Come, help me pack damp sand to strengthen the left turret."

They worked together in companionable silence for several minutes before Sandor crowed, "This sandcastle is the best we ever built, is it not?"

Jenny felt a rush of fierce maternal love. "One of the best, I agree," she equivocated with a warm smile.

A small ruckus in the vicinity of the glassed-in back porch, which spanned the width of the cottage and which served as the children's nursery, drew Jenny's eye. Birdie and Meg emerged from inside, each holding a twin's hand. Obviously the boys had woke from their naps eager to make up for lost time. Watching, Jenny didn't know whether to laugh or cry. In their enthusiasm to join the fun, the two little hedonists were dragging their protesting nannies in their wake.

When Sandor spotted his siblings, he snorted. "Oh, bother. They'll knock it down before we get it built."

Jenny's gaze shifted to her eldest son. He was too young to understand that sandcastles were transitory. Or that if the twins didn't flatten it, the relentless tide would.

"Better the twins than Attila the Hun."

"Attila the who?"

Jenny looked at Sandor's bewildered face and burst out laughing. "Never mind," she advised as she ruffled his fluffy yellow hair.

Getting no response to his firm knock but too stubborn to retreat empty-handed, Andrew walked round the cottage to the back terrace. Off in the distance, he saw the choppy waters of the English Channel, whereas the middle ground featured a cove created by a stone breakwater which provided a buffer for small craft anchored within its boundaries. However, it was the immediate foreground that commanded the bulk of his interest.

Squinting into the sun, Andrew observed two women, each with a child in hand, walking toward a third, who knelt near the borderline that separated dry sand from wet. Although the kneeling woman's back faced him, Andrew assumed she was Jenny, since he'd already identified Birdie and Meg. The third child, a sturdy-looking lad crouched beside the kneeling figure, must be his eldest son.

Andrew felt almost as if he were viewing an animated portrait. He hesitated to call attention to his presence because he feared his intrusion might spoil the idyllic harmony. Yet a nagging niggle of curiosity made him wish the kneeling woman would turn to face him so that he could be certain she was Jenny.

Nonetheless, when he noticed that the nurses were being dragged across the sand by their respective charges, he felt obliged to rescue them. Once he'd closed the distance, he saw that the two boys were as alike as peas in a pod and felt it safe to assume they were his identical twin sons, Aubrey and Alistair.

Chuckling, he asked, "Need some help, Birdie?"

The elderly nurse jumped several inches off the ground. She also loosened her grip. The freed child raced toward the kneeling woman, who greeted him with a spontaneous hug even as Birdie whirled round to face Andrew.

Arms akimbo, she scolded, "Shame on you, Master Andrew. You scared me so bad I let go of Aubrey's hand."

"Yes, that was ill done of me. But at least there's no harm done. He's safe as houses with his mother."

At that moment, Alistair managed to slip from Meg's relaxed grasp. He sprinted toward the kneeling woman, who gave Aubrey a dismissive pat on his rump before rising with grace and turning to confront her other son.

As he witnessed the unfolding tableau, Andrew

could not have moved a muscle if his life depended upon it. Nor could he speak. He was too astonished at seeing Mrs. Shaw when he'd expected to see Jenny.

His mind teemed with questions. Chief amongst them were: Whatever had possessed Mrs. Shaw and Jenny to switch places? What right did the Incomparable have romping with his sons on the beach? And where the hell was Jenny?

It simply didn't make sense. Unless, of course, he'd suddenly gone mad.

"Dearest Mama, who is that man?" Sandor asked loudly.

The instant Andrew heard Sandor address Mrs. Shaw as "dearest Mama" it was as if the scales impairing his vision had been peeled from his eyes. The selfsame Mrs. Shaw he'd met at Covent Garden merged in his mind's eye with his wife Jenny. The revelation rocked Andrew to his very core, even as he continued to stare at her in mute disbelief. For his latest hypothesis was preposterous. It was utterly impossible that his clumsy, homely, pudgy wife could have become the svelte Incomparable standing before him.

On the other hand, he had heard Sandor call Mrs. Shaw "dearest Mama." So either he'd actually gone mad or . . . or else, this woman, whoever she was, had decided to make a May-game of him. Andrew doubled his fists as a spurt of righteous indignation at the cruel hoax threatened to consume him.

"Jenny?" he asked hoarsely.

The golden-eyed beauty looked almost as startled as he felt. Her welcoming smile vanished so swiftly, Andrew couldn't be sure he'd actually seen it or if it had been a figment of his imagination. Frozen to the spot, he watched her complexion grow steadily paler. So pale he feared she'd either faint or fade completely away before his very eyes.

"You're not my wife. You can't be," he said.

"Yes, I am. I'm Jenny," she said, her calm voice at odds with her pallor.

"Do you take me for a fool? You're Mrs. Shaw. Where's Jenny? By God, if you've harmed a hair on her head, you'll answer to me."

"Don't be silly. Jenny's fine. That is, *I* am fine. Only consider: because you don't recognize me doesn't mean I'm not who I claim to be."

"Madam, if you don't cease lying to me this instant, I'll shake the truth out of you."

"No!" cried Sandor, stepping between them.

Andrew peered into his son's anguished face and felt his heart turn over. Paternal pride in the boy's courage warred with consternation at what a fool he was to let his frustration get out of hand. By harassing the woman Alexander regarded as his mother, Andrew had not only presented himself in a poor light, he'd forced his three-year-old son to leap to her defense.

Andrew could only applaud the lovely impostor's good sense when she appealed to the children's nurses. "Birdie, Meg, our conversation is distressing the children. Please take them inside."

"That I will, my lady. And none too soon neither!"

Birdie sent Andrew a dark look that clearly threatened retribution unless he minded his p's and q's. She took hold of each twin's hand. She began to trudge through the sand toward the cottage. After a few furtive glances in his direction, the twins went with her without a murmur of protest.

Perfectly understandable given the circumstances, Andrew supposed. All three boys regarded him, not as their father, but as a complete stranger. No wonder the twins were suddenly so docile. He'd scared the hell out of them. He felt sick to his stomach. Fool that he was, he'd made mincemeat of what he'd hoped would be a happy family reunion. Clearly he would have to tread more carefully if he hoped to win his sons' affection.

So much for future plans. Right now, a tenaciously stubborn loose end loomed. While the twins retreated like docile lambs, Sandor refused to budge, despite the soft entreaties offered by the woman the boy regarded as his mother.

Whoever she was, at least her motives were sound, Andrew reflected. They could not speak freely in the boy's presence, because to do so would clearly disturb Sandor, who was too young not to be frightened by a heated discussion. Mentally crossing his fingers, Andrew hunkered down beside the boy.

"Sandor, do you know who I am?" he asked gently.

"No, sir."

"Well, I am your father and I need to talk to the lady you are so gallantly shielding. Now then, speaking man to man, if I promise not to harm a hair on her head, will you agree to go along quietly with Meg?"

"I don't know if I should. You could be lying."

"I could be, but I am not."

Catching Sandor's look of skepticism, Andrew sensed the boy was wavering and gave a mirthless chuckle. "Very well, King Solomon, take a moment to weigh things."

Jenny placed her hand on Sandor's rigid shoulder and squeezed gently. "Son, your father has given you his word. I think you should trust him."

"But, Mama, he yelled at you."

"Yes, well, sometimes grownups lose their tempers. But consider this: I've known your father longer than you have, and I trust him to keep his word. Now, please go with Meg."

The boy reflected a moment. "Birdie was his nurse when he was a boy. That's how he knows her name, but how does he know Meg's?"

Andrew smiled at the boy's cleverness. "Because I hired her before you could crawl to help Birdie keep track of you. Now, young man, I suggest you run along before you and I come to cuffs."

Sandor gazed at him intently. Andrew held his

breath. He felt as if his integrity was indeed being weighed by King Solomon himself. Evidently satisfied at what he saw in his father's gaze, the boy shot him a shy grin, then scampered off toward the cottage. Dipping a curtsy, Meg followed.

Overhead, a gull cried out as if in mortal pain as Andrew trained cold, wary eyes upon his beautiful adversary.

"Madam, I fear I've lost track of the exact plateau reached in our quarrel. Suffice to say, I regard you as an impostor. I'm sick of your lies and demand you tell me the truth."

"Truth? You want the truth?"

Andrew returned her fulminating glare with interest. "I most certainly do."

"Very well, sir, you shall have it." Anger flared to life in her eyes as she looked straight into his and said, "The truth is I'm both."

"Both? Both?" To Andrew's disgust, he could hear himself echoing her outrageous claim like a demented parrot. "Impossible!"

"It matters naught whether you believe me or not. At the risk of repeating myself, I'm both Mrs. Shaw and your wife, Jenny."

"If I were you, madam, I'd choose my words with great care. For if what you claim is true, you deliberately misled me by using a false name at Covent Garden."

"I merely chose not to flaunt my married title."

Red-hot embers danced in Andrew's dark blue eyes in stark contrast to his frigid tone. "By God, did you? Then deceiving me was deliberate. How you must have enjoyed laughing up your sleeve at me."

Jenny's eyes shimmered like molten gold. "You mistake the matter, my lord," she said icily. "I assure you there is nothing the least bit amusing about being introduced to a husband who neither recognizes his own wife nor recalls her maiden name."

Andrew stared at Jenny. How dare she presume to lecture him on *his* conduct after the trick *she'd* pulled at Covent Garden? How could he be expected to recall her maiden name when they'd only met minutes before they were wed? Or recognize her when her appearance had altered so dramatically? Just like a woman, she was being utterly unreasonable.

Never in his life had he felt so asea. To be told the breathtakingly lovely Mrs. Shaw was actually Jenny was mind-boggling. Surely this fiery virago could not be his sweet-natured wife.

But this willful beauty had to be who she claimed to be, because Birdie would never dream of entrusting his sons to an impostor. Equally obvious, if she was really Jenny, then more than her looks had changed.

Andrew's brow knit. No doubt his prolonged absence, coupled with his father's death six months past, had left Jenny rudderless. She'd had no man to guide her or to assume responsibilities more suited to the male gender. Thus, he could hardly blame her for assuming command. He felt it imperative, however, that he reassert his authority.

"Madam, my recollection of your maiden name would have scarcely been necessary if you'd behaved with propriety and used your married title."

Jenny glared at him. "Do you actually have the gall to throw propriety in my face after your involvement in the Quinlan divorce? I'll have you know reassuming my maiden name was your father's doing. I'd just recovered from a serious illness when he brought me here to convalesce. He thought to shield me from the scandalmongers."

Touched on the raw, Andrew felt a wave of searing heat rise inch by inch from his scorched neck until it suffused his stern countenance. With the benefit of hindsight, he now recognized that his liaison with Lady Quinlan had been sheer folly. Even so, he'd be damned if he'd let his wife lecture him on that or any other subject.

"By God, madam, now that I'm home for good, I intend to see that you toe the mark. Order the servants to pack your trunks. Henceforth, you and the boys will reside with me at Halpern Abbey."

Eyes blazing with defiance, Jenny placed her hands on her hips. "I, sir, have no intention of budging. I am not a shiny new toy to be taken up when it amuses you, only to be cast aside once something or someone else captures your fancy."

Stung to the quick, Andrew retaliated, "Allow me to point out that if you are Jenny as you claim to be, then you are also my wife. A person subject by law to obey my commands."

Trembling with fury, Jenny dug in her heels. How dare he try to order her about after leaving her to fend for herself for years on end? Well, she wouldn't stand for it. She was no longer a shy young maiden eager to bend to his will.

"Allow me to refresh your memory. We agreed to live apart once I'd borne your heir. Since I've presented you with not one, but three sons, I've more than fulfilled my part of the bargain. Make no mistake. This time round, I intend to hold you to the terms agreed to before we were wed."

Having spoken her piece, Jenny spun on her heel and fled toward the cottage before he could stop her.

At first, Andrew resented her haste since it denied him a chance to launch a rebuttal, but once he'd cooled off, he was almost glad she'd left before he'd foolishly attempted to trump her queen with his king without first being privy to all the facts.

His lean, aristocratic features grew pensive. At present, he was more or less groping in the dark. All sorts of questions milled around in his head, each needing an answer. He'd known Birdie from the cradle and trusted her implicitly. Knowledge was power. Before he confronted Jenny again, he needed to speak to his former nanny.

Seventeen

Andrew sent word to the nursery that he wished to see Birdie. Ten minutes later, she shuffled into the enclosed sun porch, grumbling about her lumbago. Her bent form brought a lump to Andrew's throat, for the curvature of her spine had grown more pronounced during his absence. Indeed, the only part of Birdie's anatomy that appeared impervious to the ravages of time were her alert blue eyes that never seemed to lose their snap or sparkle.

Andrew frowned. Had the added stress of caring for three lively youngsters contributed to her physical deterioration? He suspected it had. Clearly his decision to bring Birdie out of retirement to oversee his nursery had been unpardonably selfish, yet he'd known no one else he could trust to keep an eye on things. Perhaps now it would be a kindness to pension her off, Andrew reflected as she settled her brittle bones into a Queen Anne chair.

Silence stretched before them like a distant horizon. Always before he'd been able to confide in

Birdie. Now, for the first time ever, he sensed an invisible barrier stood between them.

"I've so many questions, I don't know where to start," he confessed with a disarming grin.

"Anyplace will do."

"Very well. Any idea what changed my homely wife into a beauty?"

Birdie's expression turned stony. "She were always a beauty inside where it counts. You were just too blind to see it."

His bewilderment mirrored in his dark blue gaze, Andrew asked quietly, "Birdie, have I offended you in some way?"

"Since you ask, the shabby way you've treated your wife puts me all out of patience. As to what changed her, I be happy to tell you. M'lady were not quite up to snuff after birthing twins when in waltzes diphtheria to knock the poor lamb off her pins."

"That much I know. Dr. Ellers filled me in."

"Oh? Did he tell you she near died?"

"Yes, but she didn't die, did she?" he said steadily.

"No. But it left her bald."

"She got better though. And her hair grew back in, too, didn't it, Birdie?"

"Aye. Only thicker and a mite darker. Changed her looks some."

Andrew raised an eyebrow. "Some? Her new crop of hair is nothing short of glorious. Her eyebrows and eyelashes are darker. Did they fall out as well?"

Birdie nodded. "Grew back black as pitch. Brings out the gold in her eyes."

"So I've noticed. I gather she lost her pudginess at the same time?"

"By no means. Food turned her stomach the first few months she carried the twins. Lost more weight than she could afford. More's the pity. A little extra padding might've come in handy when she caught diphtheria."

The sensitive skin at his nape prickled. Birdie blamed him for Jenny's illness, which was crazy. It crossed his mind that perhaps she'd grown a tad senile. But one problem at a time.

Andrew smiled. He could just imagine Birdie's reaction if he broke down and confessed that he missed Jenny's elfin exuberance, a trait that had prompted him to nickname her "sprite" during their honeymoon. Birdie would think his wits were addled. But dammit, he missed his sprite.

"Don't get me wrong. The change in Jenny's appearance pleases me. What troubles me is the change I see in her nature."

"Oh? Sticks in your craw that she stands up to you now, do it?"

Andrew checked a frown. Obviously winning Birdie's support was going to be an uphill battle.

"Actually, I don't mind being challenged on occasion. It's just that the wife I left behind was sweeter and more eager to please. Frankly, I miss her and was hoping you could tell me how to coax her back."

"Fustian! Iffen I knew, I'd never open me mummer—not for a million pounds. You don't want a wife, you want a doormat."

"That's an unfair assumption. I don't mind that she's acquired some gumption. It's just that I miss her sweetness."

"M'lord, when you turned your back on her, she were increasing. So if she be more tart than sweet now, you've only yourself to blame." Wagging her finger at him, Birdie resumed her tirade. "And iffen she no longer falls all over you like an eager puppy, 'tis only what you deserve."

Andrew flinched. His cheek stung as if the nanny he'd always loved and trusted had slapped him. Not since his nursery days had he felt so unworthy.

The message in Birdie's eyes was crystal clear: *Shame on you. I raised you better. I taught you to behave better. I expected more from you.*

Andrew dropped his head into his hands. Always before, he'd been able to count on Birdie's support. Now she'd switched loyalties and stood firmly in Jenny's corner, and that hurt like the dickens. But what hurt the most was having to admit to himself that he'd deserved Birdie's shattering set-down.

Yet even though his remorse ran deep, Andrew knew he must resist the temptation to wallow in self-pity. He needed to redeem himself. Birdie was too shrewd to be taken in by empty promises. Only worthy deeds would placate her.

Common sense told him he must try to attain his goals through gentle persuasion. If it worked, fine. If it didn't, he had an ace up his sleeve to fall back on. Because, if worse came to worst, all he need do to gain a biddable wife was to threaten to remove the boys from Jenny's household. Such drastic action was completely within his rights. Indeed, any court in the land would uphold his decision. Still, Andrew had no wish to break Jenny's spirit. Besides, resorting to such an ignoble tactic would not only further alienate Birdie, it would further entrench Jenny's animosity toward him.

Truth be told, while he'd grown deuced fond of Jenny during the months they'd spent together before he'd left for Russia, he'd had little respect for her. Now that she'd put some steel in her backbone, he did.

Most disturbing to his peace of mind, Jenny's challenge that he live up to their bargain contained a subtle reminder that he hadn't always done so in the past. Thus, if he wanted to regain both her affection and her respect, if he wanted to mend the breach between them, he must not resort to coercion. Far better, he reasoned, to use his considerable powers of persuasion, honed to perfection during his diplomatic career, to wear her down.

Several weeks later, Jenny slipped quietly into the nursery where Andrew was reading all three boys a bedtime story. The cozy scene tugged on her heartstrings. Admittedly, at first she'd balked at granting him unlimited access to her three sons. But once she'd calmed down enough to consider the benefits, her attitude had undergone a dramatic change. Consequently when he'd requested permission to read them a bedtime story on alternate nights, she'd felt it would have been unreasonable to refuse, and foolhardy as well. No matter how many times she defended her position by citing the terms of their prenuptial bargain, the fact remained that her husband's authority over her sons, or herself for that matter, ranked supreme in the eyes of the law.

Undeniably her peace of mind had been sorely strained by Andrew's unexpected appearance on her doorstep. Her mistaken belief that she couldn't be easily traced had lulled her into a false sense of security. Her assumption that she'd have several more years to enjoy her sons' exclusive company had proved to be erroneous.

Thank goodness Andrew had had the tact to rent a nearby cottage rather than insist upon living under the same roof. And thank goodness he'd changed his tactics and ceased to play tyrant.

Fortunately for all, she'd identified her initial negative response to his request that she share the children with him as jealousy, pure and simple. Even more fortunate, once she'd seen how much the boys delighted in his company, her jealousy had swiftly evaporated and she'd been able to concede that Andrew's fatherhood skills could not be faulted. Still, only time would tell if he were truly interested in forming close, permanent

onds with his sons or was merely amused by the
novelty of fatherhood. The latter possibility made
Jenny want to cry. Instead, she gave her full attention to the four males in her life.

Like clockwork, on alternate nights, Andrew
showed up to read the boys a bedtime story. More
rarely, he related suitably censored accounts of
his travels or told them a Russian folk tale.

Tonight, he was reading *Dick Whittington and
his Cat* to them. The indisputably English tale was
one of their favorites, and Jenny was amused to
find that both her husband and her sons were so
caught up in the story, they never noticed her
slip quietly into the room. The longer she listened to Andrew recite the rhymed verses, the
broader her smile at the heartwarming scene.
Alistair and Aubrey flanked each of their father's
sides while Sandor clung to his back, his thin
arms draped round his father's neck.

> "To Holloway he walked, when lo!
> He heard the merry bells of Bow:
> In Richard's ear they seemed to chime
> This uncouth, strange and simple rhyme:
> 'Turn again, Whittington,
> 'Thrice Lord Mayor of London.' "

When Andrew closed the book with a decisive
snap, the twins fixed pleading eyes upon their
father and tried to wheedle him into reading
"just one more story."

"No, it's bedtime. However, either your mother

or I will read you another tomorrow night, pro
vided you don't kick up a fuss."

Andrew awarded Jenny such a warm glance
she suspected he'd known of her presence ever
though he hadn't given the slightest sign. "Here'
your mother come to tuck you in and kiss you
good night."

Since Meg had been granted leave to spend th
night with her ailing mother and Birdie had
looked so worn out from trying to keep up with
three lively youngsters all day, it was up to Jenny
to see her sons settled for the night.

"Easier said than done," she grumbled a half
hour later as she preceded her husband from th
nursery.

Andrew's fingertips exerted just enough pres
sure upon the small of her back to guide her
down a narrow passage. On one hand, Jenny ap
preciated his courteous gesture. On the other, she
wished he'd keep his hands to himself, since hi
touch stirred up sensations that she'd prefer to
let slumber.

His fingertips continued to graze the satin ma
terial of her dinner gown as they entered the in
formal sitting room. Jenny's pulse quickened, and
her mouth and throat suddenly went dry. She
managed a painful swallow, which failed to alle
viate her discomfort. At least a cheerful fire, ca
pable of warding off the night chill present along
the Devon coastline even in summer, burned on
the hearth. It gave her an excuse to bolt out of
arm's reach.

Andrew frowned as he watched Jenny scuttle toward the hearth. Weeks ago he'd instituted a regimen of casual touches in the hope of gradually reawakening Jenny's passion. So far, his scheme didn't seem to be working.

Masking his frustration, he crossed to the hearth. Jenny promptly retreated to a nearby wing chair. With an inward sigh, he consoled himself with the hopeful crumb that at least she was not totally indifferent to his touch, else she wouldn't be at such pains to avoid it.

Andrew leaned against the mantelpiece with feigned nonchalance that skillfully hid his inner tension. "My dear, did I hear you grumble as we escaped the nursery?"

Jenny gave him a rueful smile. "You did. Birdie warned me that those three scamps were at their worst just before they popped off for the night. Silly me. I thought she was exaggerating."

Andrew laughed. It had taken two glasses of water apiece, plus their mother's bribe of a picnic on the morrow, plus Andrew's sternest look before all three lads had finally settled for the night.

" 'Tis no laughing matter. Look at me. I'm ages younger than Birdie and even though you lent me a hand, I'm worn to a frazzle."

"Hmm. Perhaps we should raise her salary. What do you think?"

Even as he spoke, Andrew took brazen advantage of her invitation to look his fill. Tonight Jenny was a vision in shimmery amber satin. Its color served to emphasize the golden flecks in her irises. Furthermore, she moved with such grace, he found it hard to believe that as a new bride she'd been inclined to trip over her own feet. What's more, her dinner dress clung enticingly to lush breasts that, unless memory played him false, were fuller than formerly—no doubt the result of nursing twins. Regardless of the reason, he wanted to fondle them. Indeed, his desire to touch her was so intense, he felt in danger of going up in flames. God help him, how he ached to possess her!

"Jenny?"

His voice, a cross between a growl and a whimper, put her on guard.

"Yes, what is it?"

Coming to stand in front of her chair, he pulled her to her feet and took hold of one of her hands. A shiver raced up her spine as he gently massaged her thumb. His expressive dark blue eyes seemed to promise the moon.

"I want you. I need you. Let me stay with you tonight."

Her pulse pounding in her ears, Jenny snatched her hand back. "No!" she cried, then said more softly, "No."

Her answer must be no even though, God help her, she wanted him every bit as badly as he did her. Indeed, she'd never stopped wanting him. Just as she'd never stopped loving him. Still, it had been such a long time since he'd touched her intimately. Jenny needed to be held close. She

eeded him to make exquisite love to her, yet she
ared not admit it.

"No? How can you be so stubborn. How can
ou tell me no if you care for me at all. Don't
ou see? I burn for you. Be reasonable."

Jenny shook her head. She was no longer a
ool. Once before he'd maneuvered her into bed
y implying that he was ready to shuck their
riginal agreement for one of permanency—only
o coldly claim that she'd mistaken his intent once
e'd tired of her charms. Once before she'd
rusted him, only to have him break his word in
pirit, if not in fact. Once before she'd given him
er heart and he'd broken it. Never again.

"You deserted me once. What assurance do I
ave that you won't do so again?" she asked
oolly.

"Because I've resigned from the diplomatic
orp. Because I've inherited a fresh set of respon-
ibilities along with the title. Because I want to
levote more time to my wife and sons. Trust me.
'm home for good."

"Trust you? I wish I could. But I don't. Nor
an I be sure I ever will again." She looked away.

Jenny knew Andrew thought she was just being
tubborn. She knew her continued refusal to re-
nove to Halpern Abbey rankled. Just as her re-
usal to let him bed her put his nose out of joint.
The trouble was no matter what he said, she
wasn't sure she could trust him. Once before he'd
urt her badly. Why give him another chance?

In response to the dinner gong, Andrew took

firm possession of his wife's elbow and led he
into the dining room. Stubborn wench! h
brooded. He wanted her so badly, though, he'd
do almost anything to win her. He couldn't risl
losing her.

Make no mistake! thought Andrew as he dippec
a soup spoon into the chilled consommé Soame:
set before him. Convincing an older, wiser Jenny
of anything whatsoever was a challenge. Indeed
arguing with her had proved so exhausting, he
hadn't had any energy left to crow when he'd fi
nally convinced her the boys would benefit from
his company and had gained her consent to spend
more time with them.

Rising, Andrew informed Jenny of his decisior
to forgo the dubious privilege of sitting alone a
the table swilling port instead of joining her immediately in the sitting room. When she offerec
no demur, he regarded her thoughtfully.

The maid he'd insisted upon hiring to attend
her had braided her mistress's dark honey hair
and arranged it in a coronet. And as he drew
back Jenny's chair, he noted several wispy curls
had escaped from the plaited crown. Curls that
brushed like delicate butterfly wings against the
baby-soft skin at the nape of Jenny's neck. Tender
skin just begging to be kissed. Sensitized skin he
ached to touch.

Andrew stifled a groan. Why must she oppose
him at every turn. How much more of this tor-
ment could he stand? True, he'd won the latest
battle and now dined with her nightly, yet he

ould by no means rest on his laurels. Not while
he still shrank from even his most casual touch.
Not while he continued to burn for her.

Surely, he told himself, there must be some way
o persuade Jenny to give him another chance.

Eighteen

"I'm sorry I was naughty, Mama. Do you still love me?"

"Of course I love you. I always will. What I do not love is bad conduct. I know your brothers sometimes make you cross, but that's no excuse to hit them."

"How else can I keep them out of my things?"

"By telling Birdie or Meg."

"I did that first."

"I see. Well, tell me next time. Now you may go, provided you promise to stop hitting your brothers."

"I'll try, Mama."

"See that you do, young man," she said sternly.

Watching him race off, Jenny had to smile. With only three-and-a-half years on his plate, Sandor had sense enough not to make a promise he suspected he couldn't keep.

Andrew collided with his heir when both of them tried to cross the threshold from opposite directions. Setting the boy back on his feet, he asked, "Where are you off to in such a hurry?"

"To lunch, Papa. May I be excused? I don'

want to miss out on my share of custard pudding."

Andrew laughed. "We can't have that, can we? Run along then, only this time mind where you're going."

Observing the love and mutual respect that passed between father and son, Jenny felt her inner resistance slowly turn to mush. The children trusted Andrew. And from the bottom of her yearning heart, she wished she could bring herself to trust him, too.

Andrew entered and shut the door behind him. Jenny sighed. Her husband called these private exchanges reasoned discussions. Jenny called them arguments. Arguments that never failed to tie her stomach in knots.

"My dear, I've enjoyed our long holiday at the seashore. But autumn approaches and I must soon return to Halpern Abbey. When I do, I want you and the children to accompany me. Will you come, Jenny?"

Her golden eyes clouded. God knew she wanted to say yes, but what she yearned for was Andrew's love, and she was no longer willing to settle for anything less.

She shook her head. "I'd like to oblige you, but given present circumstances, I cannot."

Andrew clenched his fists. Her refusal infuriated him. For weeks on end, he hadn't put a foot wrong. For weeks on end, he'd exercised patience. For weeks on end, he'd tried to woo her. He'd brought her flowers, bonbons, books, fans, and other fripperies. Times without number, he'd waxed eloquent regarding her beauty and flattered her with shameless abandon. What else could he do? What more could she want? What more could she expect from him?

"Jenny, I've bent over backward trying to please you. Must you be so stubborn? You never used to be."

She glared at him. "I was only seventeen when we were wed. I didn't have sense enough to stand up for my rights. Now I do."

"Your rights?" Andrew exploded. "Madam, you go too far. I'm sick and tired of trying to placate you. Sick and tired of you opposing me at every turn. If you refuse to see reason, I shall resort to harsher measures. Rights? In the eyes of the law, you have no rights. But I do. If I wish, it is my right to wrench your children from your tender breast."

Jenny stamped her foot. "My lord, I beg you to cease ranting and raging."

Her rebuke stung. Andrew bowed stiffly. "I beg your pardon. I didn't intend to shout. I lost my temper."

"Apology accepted. But to return to our discussion, I know you have the right to not only remove my sons from this cottage but also—should you choose to exercise it—the right to deny me all access to them until they are grown.

"But I beg leave to remind you that we both agreed to honor the terms of a bargain drawn up before we married. Furthermore, you took pains to spell out *your* interpretation of the terms it encompassed just before you hared off to Russia. You promised our children would live with me until school age and, from that time on, agreed to alternate their holidays.

"One reason I hesitate to accompany you to the Abbey is that, as a young bride, I trusted you implicitly. You let me down by first storming my defenses and then abandoning me to face the consequences alone. You did not even have the courtesy to respond to my letter advising you of the twins' birth. How could you be so heartless?"

Andrew visibly paled. "Jenny, had I got your letter, you may be sure I'd have answered it. But Silas Minton took it upon himself to forward your letter to me by surface mail instead of via diplomatic pouch. Considering the chaotic conditions once Bonaparte invaded Russia, 'tis not too surprising that I never received it. To be sure, I've raked Minton over the coals for his singular lapse of judgment the instant I found out about it."

Jenny stared at him thoughtfully. "I must say it's quite a relief to learn you are not as black as I'd painted you. However, my chief concern is the immediate present. Andrew, what does your latest threat imply? Are you telling me you intend to renege on our prenuptial bargain yet again?"

Andrew felt as if suddenly all his fingers had turned into thumbs. Whatever had become of his noteworthy address that had helped smooth the way during the course of his diplomatic career? he wondered.

"Forget what I said. I spoke in anger. I wouldn't dream of separating you from the boys."

"Wretch!"

"You are not easily intimidated. I admire that."

Andrew responded to Jenny's unladylike snort with a wry chuckle that in turn raised her hackles.

"This is no laughing matter," she said bitingly.

Sober-faced, he said, "I agree. Indeed, it is only fair to warn you that while I shall take pains not to infringe on the terms of our infamous bargain, since obviously any further tampering will sink me beyond the pale, I intend to use every weapon in my arsenal to persuade you to winter with me at Halpern Abbey."

"And you dare call me stubborn?" Jenny scoffed. "Give over, Andrew. I shall not budge."

Andrew's lips thinned. "Have a care, Jenny. Else you'll force me to adopt more stringent measures. For instance, I could break the lease on this cottage, leaving you no other choice but to accompany me to Sticklepath."

Her eyes raked him up and down. "Another idle threat, my lord?"

"By no means," he riposted. " 'Ware, my sweet, lest you end up without a roof over your lovely head."

"Your threat has no teeth. There is no lease. I own the cottage free and clear."

"Damnation!" he exploded.

"Quite," snapped Jenny. "Now if this discussion is over, I beg to be excused."

"Ah, but it is not over. I've merely fired a warning shot across your bow. I have the right to your property, including the right to dispose of it. By law, I can sell this cottage right out from under you if I so choose."

The golden eyes glittered. "I think not. Your father made careful arrangements, something on the order of a trust deed I believe, to insure that I am the sole owner."

To further indicate her disdain for his latest threat, Jenny yawned. Her deliberate goad drove Andrew's temper to fever pitch.

"By all that's holy, if you don't cease to bait me, I'll turn you over my knee."

Jenny responded with a look of feigned pity. "A diplomat resorting to violence? Shame on you, sir."

"Madam, don't tempt me," Andrew advised through gritted teeth. "While, thanks to my father's meddling, it may well be beyond my power to sell this cottage, I do have the right to cut off your quarterly stipend. When your children grow hungry, you'll have no recourse but to bow to my wishes."

"My lord, foolish bluster does not become you. I am not blind. You dote on your sons. Do you actually expect me to believe you'd let them suffer? But even if you resort to such a drastic measure, they won't starve. Your father willed me a small annuity."

"So that's how you managed to feed three sons on an allowance meant for one."

"Precisely."

Andrew gazed at Jenny in wonder. For the first time since he'd reached his majority, he felt a niggling doubt that perhaps he wasn't going to get his way.

Wait a minute! Even supposing Jenny were capable of stretching every single penny of her limited resources, how did that square with the lovely vision he'd run across at Covent Garden? How on earth could she afford such a fashionable—not to mention expensive—gown? Andrew relished his chance to cross-examine his lovely, albeit maddeningly recalcitrant, wife.

"All those lovely gowns you ordered from your London dressmaker. How did you pay for them?"

The stunned look on Jenny's face was priceless.

"Madam, am I to assume from your silence that I'm about to be dunned for them?" he asked silkily.

Jenny's golden irises flashed fiery sparks. "Certainly not. I paid for them with my advance against royalties."

Andrew's mouth fell open. "Royalties?"

Jenny nodded. "For my book on botany."

Beneath his feet, the world tilted crazily. "Let me get this straight. You actually wrote a book? On botany?"

Her eyes sparkled with triumph. "You look surprised."

"Surprised? My dear, Jenny, I'm flabbergasted.

Whatever made you decide to take on such an onerous task?"

"Oh, I didn't. At least not intentionally. I compiled my collection of wildflower sketches simply because it gave me pleasure. But after your father died, I realized, while the funds at my disposal would provide the necessities, there'd be precious little left over for emergencies or an occasional treat for the boys."

Jenny tossed him a mischievous glance. "Or for an occasional stylish gown to shore up my spirits. So, I put my sketches in proper order, added a few lines of text beneath each drawing, and shipped off the lot. In April, my publisher wrote to say his firm wished to publish my manuscript, and I traveled up to London to discuss the terms of my contract."

Still a bit dazed, he said, "So that's what brought you to Town."

"Yes. Yesterday, I received word from my publisher that *The Portable Flower Garden* has sold out and that he's going to print a second edition."

"It's already published?"

"Oh, yes. My first royalty check should arrive any day."

"I see.. Do you perchance have a copy handy?"

"Of course."

Jenny removed a leather-bound book from the shelf and handed it to Andrew. He leafed through the folio, his breath catching in his throat as he gazed at the exquisitely executed sketches.

Emotions in turmoil, he said, "My dear, this is an outstanding collection. You can be justly proud of yourself. Indeed, I am extremely proud that you are my marchioness."

Jenny looked incredulous. "Your marchioness?"

"Why, yes. Since you are married to me, the title is rightfully yours."

"I'm aware of that. But I had no idea that you regarded me in that light."

"Well, of course, I do. You are, after all, my wife. And now that we've cleared up that misunderstanding, what do you say to taking your rightful place beside me at Halpern Abbey this winter?"

Andrew found the expression in her lovely eyes maddeningly enigmatic. Teasing little witch, he grumbled to himself as he waited with bated breath for her answer.

"I'm not sure I'm suited to play such a role."

"Goose! Promise me you'll come."

Jenny shook her head. "I can't promise, but . . . I'll think about it."

"Yes, you do that," he replied, then let her go before he made an ass of himself and kissed her.

Once alone, Andrew sank into a chair, now at leisure to peruse the handsome folio. But finding himself too overwrought to do it justice, he soon set it aside. He was in awe of Jenny's accomplishment. To be sure, he'd known she enjoyed sketching and had encouraged her to pursue this hobby during their honeymoon. Still, it had never crossed his mind that she might be so talented.

Come to that, he'd never, even for a moment, considered her to be his equal. Neither had he respected her. Nor perceived her as desirable. So, that last recrimination could be struck. Andrew had, indeed, found her desirable, a fact that had puzzled him at the time.

Conceited ass that he was, he'd been too preoccupied with his own ambitions to bother to delve beneath the homely surface. True, he'd found her awkwardness somewhat endearing. Indeed, he'd dubbed her "sprite" because her irrepressible exuberance never failed to pull him out of the doldrums. Nonetheless, the unpalatable truth was he'd treated his own wife with the careless affection he might bestow upon a clumsy puppy that amused him.

Andrew emitted a tortured sigh. To be candid, he regarded his wife's published folio as a mixed blessing. Thus, while his chest had swelled with pride when he'd thumbed through her book, he'd also experienced a poignant sadness. By foolishly distancing himself from Jenny early in their marriage, he'd forced her to fend for herself. And, to her credit, she'd emerged from her trial by fire as a lovely, confident woman who no longer needed a man to protect her or to fight her battles.

Ironically, he'd received his just deserts. It was his own damned fault that Jenny continued to regard him with wary eyes. His bride had come to him starry-eyed, only to have him carelessly abandon her on the flimsy excuse that she *might*

embarrass him if allowed to move in diplomati
circles.

He positively loathed that sanctimonious pri
he'd been three years ago. He could kick himsel
for not recognizing what a gem he'd held in th
palm of his hand. He deserved an even harde
kick for not realizing he'd been in love with hi
own wife. He'd just been too blind to see it.

Restless, Andrew rose and went to stand besid
the window that overlooked the cove. Had only
half-hour passed since the moment he'd gaze
into Jenny's eyes and recognized with the awe
some force of a thunderbolt that he adored her

How ironic that he'd spurned everything h
now craved so desperately. Worst of all, he wa
by no means certain that he'd succeed in winnin
back the heart he hadn't had sense enough t
treasure when initially offered.

Jenny stared out the window while her morn
ing chocolate grew tepid. Not that she could se
much in this fog. Indeed, she could barely mak
out the wild roses climbing a trellis located onl
a few feet from the cottage.

Shivering, she wrapped her kashmir shaw
more tightly round her shoulders in a vain at
tempt to ward off the clammy dampness. Andrev
was leaving. He'd told her he was tired of fencin
with her and planned to leave as soon as Parson
finished some last-minute packing.

Jenny had her pride. Andrew had gone to th

ursery to say goodbye to the boys, and while he
remained on the premises, she'd rather die than
disgrace herself by weeping and wailing. But,
ear God, it was hard to hold back a sea of tears
threatening to spill.

Wringing her hands, Birdie shuffled into the
room. "My lady, I been looking high and low for
you."

"Have you? Is Andrew still with the boys?"

"No, he be gone. Left the nursery in an up-
oar."

"Oh? Do you want me to help restore order?"

"No, my lady. I cannot lay me hands on Master
Alexander. I hoped to find him with you."

"Well, he isn't here. Are you sure he's not hid-
ng in one of the cupboards?"

"Meg and me turned the nursery inside out.
And still nary a sign of the rascal."

"I see. How long since he turned up missing?"

"Ten minutes, more or less. Refused to give his
ather a goodbye hug. Mayhap he had a change
f heart and followed him home."

"A distinct possibility," Jenny conceded, reso-
utely ignoring the hollow sensation in the pit of
er stomach. Sandor might well be in danger,
hough. That she could not ignore.

Jenny gave the bellpull a yank. When Soames
esponded, she ordered him to send the groom
o Andrew's rented cottage three doors down the
trand. Closing her eyes, she prayed Andrew's
ravel coach hadn't driven off yet. She prayed

Birdie was right and that Sandor had run afte[r] his father. But Jenny didn't think he had.

A painful breath seared her lungs, then caugh[t] in her throat. *Sandor would head straight for th[e] breakwater. She just knew it.*

Choking back a sob, she recalled how he'[d] loved to scramble over those boulder-sized rock[s] before she'd forbidden them to him. The troubl[e] was, despite numerous scolds, he *still* went ther[e] whenever he felt overwhelmed. And one did no[t] have to be a genius to conclude that Andrew'[s] sudden departure had turned Sandor's stable worl[d] topsy-turvy.

Jenny groaned. Her son's ten-minute lead prac[-] tically guaranteed he'd reach the breakwater be[-] fore she could catch up to him. Heart thumping[,] she told Birdie where she was going and ran out[-] side. She left her shoes at the edge of the terrace[.] She could travel faster in bare feet.

Jenny sprinted along the shoreline on damp[,] hard-packed sand. Sandor could barely kee[p] afloat—let alone swim. Her heart skipped, the[n] accelerated as she reached the breakwater and be[-] gan to climb. Should Sandor chance to step o[n] a clump of the slippery seaweed that clung to th[e] boulders, he might tumble into the sea.

Frustrated, she cursed the thick fog that se[-] verely limited her vision. Her next thought struc[k] terror in her heart. *Her son could be only a few fee[t] away and she'd never know it! Not unless she ra[n] across him accidentally.*

Tears clogged her throat. She swallowed them[.]

his was no time for tears. The fog might impair
er vision, but there was nothing wrong with her
oice. Shouting her son's name, Jenny inched for-
ard.

Jenny's scalp prickled. Wonder of wonders, she
eard Andrew shouting her name. Unfortunately,
he'd long since yelled herself hoarse and could
nly respond with a weak croak. She could not
e certain she'd made herself heard, although it
id seem to her that he was drawing nearer.

She nibbled on her lower lip. Irony of ironies,
he fate she'd feared would be Sandor's was now
ers. She, not Sandor, had lost her footing.
Which wasn't to say that she'd tumbled into the
ea and drowned. Still, Andrew had better move
uickly, because Jenny was literally hanging by
er fingertips from the jagged outcropping just
bove.

To her horror, a piece of the ledge she clung
o broke off in her hand. Jenny gave a startled
queak. *Lord save her! She now dangled from one
rm!*

In bare feet, Andrew leapt from boulder to
oulder. He'd damned near had heart failure
when Birdie told him that Jenny had gone to the
reakwater to look for Sandor.

Come to that, his heartbeat was still erratic,
ince he knew Jenny couldn't swim. He'd found

that out when she'd tumbled into the brook dur
ing their honeymoon. Leaping to the next boul
der, Andrew decided to take advantage of
momentary gap in the fog bank to peer down a
the base of the breakwater where icy Channel
waters surrounded a scattering of jagged rock for
mations.

A shudder wracked his wiry frame. If Jenn
should lose her balance and fall from this heigh
she'd be lucky if she didn't break her neck. H
must find her at once despite the thick curtai
of fog that hindered his progress. By midday i
would have blown inland, but that was no hel
to him now. He leapt across a wide chasm to th
next boulder. Sighting her, his eyes almos
popped out of their sockets.

*Jenny was hanging on to the rim of the adjacer
boulder by her fingertips!*

"Holy hell!" he exclaimed.

"Andrew?" Jenny croaked.

"Hang on, sweetheart. I'm coming."

But when he jumped onto the boulder sh
clung to, it jiggled and Jenny lost her tenuou
grip. Her scream echoed and re-echoed in An
drew's ears as she fell into the choppy sea.

"Holy hell!" he muttered and dove in after her

Scant minutes ago, Jenny had been so cold he
teeth chattered, but now the sun had broke
through the clouds and felt deliciously warm o
her eyelids.

"Welcome back, sweetheart."

Jenny opened her eyes and saw Andrew on the each next to her. "Sandor?"

"Is safe and sound. Naughty scamp followed ie home. When I brought him back to the cottge, Birdie told me where you'd gone."

Jenny tried to sit up, but Andrew gently re-rained her. "Lie still for a bit longer. After all ie trouble I went to to save you from drowning, refuse to let you court a relapse."

"You rescued me?"

"Yes." He frowned. "You look surprised."

"I am. Why didn't you let me drown?"

Andrew's jaw dropped. "Let you drown? Lord, hat a monster you must think me!"

"No such thing! I merely thought . . . that is, know how much you dote on the boys, and with ie gone, you'd have a clear field."

"Jenny, I suspect all that water you swallowed as temporarily addled your wits. Naturally I love iy sons, but you, my love, are my dearest treas-re."

"My lord, did your brains perchance become ater-logged during your unscheduled swim? reasure, indeed," she scoffed.

"Dearest treasure," Andrew insisted firmly. Jenny, I don't resent sharing my sons with you. ndeed, I envy their good fortune in having such caring mother."

Jenny still looked a trifle uncertain, but she nanaged a slight smile. "Very prettily said, my

lord. I thank you most sincerely for saving n
life."

"My pleasure, madam." His eyes held a teasin
light. "Believe me, it's not every day that one ge
to rescue such a beautiful siren."

Jenny had just begun to glory in the fuss An
drew was making, but the instant he said th
word *beautiful,* her hand flew to her sodden ha
and all her peace was destroyed.

"Andrew, I know you are only funning, but
mortifies me when you pretend you think m
beautiful."

"Sweetheart, if you don't shut your lovel
mouth, I shall be forced to take steps."

Jenny sighed. "No threats please. I'm not u
to your weight today. And my mouth is nc
lovely."

"Yes, it is. And you are beautiful whether yo
choose to believe it or not."

"I'm not, I'm not. Stop mocking me. It hurt
it hurts." Jenny choked back a sob.

With infinite tenderness, Andrew's arms enci
cled her. "Hush, my love," he pleaded softly.

Jenny felt too weak to struggle, and besides
felt good to be held and rocked gently until sh
quieted.

"My beautiful wife, I don't want to be rid o
you. What I want is a real marriage, not a shar
one."

Jenny groaned. The water she'd swallowed ha
not only dulled her wits, it had affected her hea
ing as well.

"A real marriage?"

Andrew gave a long sigh. "I don't know why I expected you to believe me. You never do."

The bleakness in his voice touched her. She lifted her head off his warm chest and leaned back far enough so she could study his face. What she saw astonished her.

"Andrew, are those tears I see in your eyes?"

He nodded.

"But why tears?"

"Because I almost lost you today and I find the thought insupportable. I love you, you see."

"You love me? Really?"

His mouth twitched. "Cross my heart."

"H-how long?"

"Since I first set eyes on you, only I was too blind to see it. I had no inkling of my true feelings until I came back and saw how well you'd managed without me. Stings my pride to admit it, but at the same time, I cannot help but be proud that you are my wife. Just as I cannot help but regret that I wasn't here to see you blossom.

"And, Jenny, you are beautiful. But vastly more important, you possess an inner beauty infinitely more precious than your lovely facade. Thanks to my folly, we've lost three years we might have spent together, but I am older now, Jenny, and, I trust, wiser. What I want is another chance to prove myself worthy of your regard."

"A-another chance?"

"Yes, the chance for a true and happy union. And know this, my love, if you grant me this chance, in return I will pledge my abiding love, my passion, my loyalty, my fidelity, and anything else you might care to claim."

For the first time ever, Jenny felt almost as beautiful as the wildflowers she attempted to capture on paper. Not that she believed she was actually beautiful. What she did believe was that Andrew did. Furthermore, for him to insist she was beautiful when at this particular moment she knew she looked like a drowned rat was proof positive that he was moonstruck.

"Well, my beauty, are you ready to grant me this boon, or do you intend to let me stew in my own juices a bit longer?"

"I don't quite remember your question. Would you mind repeating it?" She tossed him a saucy grin.

"Baggage! You've toyed with me long enough, madam. And if you don't answer in the affirmative this instant, I shall rain kisses on that delicious mouth until you cry mercy."

"Hmm. Is that a threat or a promise?"

"A promise," he said gruffly, then sobered. "But, Jenny, I would have your answer first."

"Very well, my lord. I will grant you another chance, but this time have a care with my heart. It's fragile."

"Yes, I know. I promise to treasure it."

"Good. Now, my lord, are you going to kiss me or not?"

"Madam, I am at your service," he growled as he slowly bent his head.

For a long while silence reigned, for both parties were fresh out of conversation and had other
pursuits in mind.

ZEBRA'S REGENCY ROMANCES
DAZZLE AND DELIGHT

A BEGUILING INTRIGUE
(4441, $3.99)

by Olivia Sumner

Pretty as a picture Justine Riggs cared nothing for propriety. She dressed as a boy, sat on her horse like a jockey, and pondered the stars like a scientist. But when she tried to best the handsome Quenton Fletcher, Marquess of Devon, by proving that she was the better equestrian, he would try to prove Justine's antics were pure folly. The game he had in mind was seduction — never imagining that he might lose his heart in the process!

AN INCONVENIENT ENGAGEMENT
(4442, $3.99)

by Joy Reed

Rebecca Wentworth was furious when she saw her betrothed waltzing with another. So she decides to make him jealous by flirting with the handsomest man at the ball, John Collinwood, Earl of Stanford. The "wicked" nobleman knew exactly what the enticing miss was up to — and he was only too happy to play along. But as Rebecca gazed into his magnificent eyes, her errant fiancé was soon utterly forgotten!

SCANDAL'S LADY
(4472, $3.99)

by Mary Kingsley

Cassandra was shocked to learn that the new Earl of Lynton was her childhood friend, Nicholas St. John. After years at sea and mixed feelings Nicholas had come home to take the family title. And although Cassandra knew her place as a governess, she could not help the thrill that went through her each time he was near. Nicholas was pleased to find that his old friend Cassandra was his new next door neighbor, but after being near her, he wondered if mere friendship would be enough . . .

HIS LORDSHIP'S REWARD
(4473, $3.99)

by Carola Dunn

As the daughter of a seasoned soldier, Fanny Ingram was accustomed to the vagaries of military life and cared not a whit about matters of rank and social standing. So she certainly never foresaw her *tendre* for handsome Viscount Roworth of Kent with whom she was forced to share lodgings, while he carried out his clandestine activities on behalf of the British Army. And though good sense told Roworth to keep his distance, he couldn't stop from taking Fanny in his arms for a kiss that made all hearts equal!

Available wherever paperbacks are sold, or order direct from the Publisher. Send cover price plus 50¢ per copy for mailing and handling to Penguin USA, P.O. Box 999, c/o Dept. 17109, Bergenfield, NJ 07621. Residents of New York and Tennessee must include sales tax. DO NOT SEND CASH.

Taylor—made Romance From Zebra Books

YOU WON'T WANT TO READ
JUST ONE — KATHERINE STONE

ROOMMATES   (3355-9, $4.95)
No one could have prepared Carrie for the monumental
changes she would face when she met her new circle of
friends at Stanford University. Once their lives intertwined
and became woven into the tapestry of the times, they would
never be the same.

TWINS   (3492-X, $4.95)
Brook and Melanie Chandler were so different, it was hard
to believe they were sisters. One was a dark, serious, ambitious New York attorney; the other, a golden, glamourous,
sophisticated supermodel. But they were more than sisters — they were twins and more alike than even they knew
. . .

THE CARLTON CLUB   (3614-0, $4.95)
It was the place to see and be seen, the only place to be. And
for those who frequented the playground of the very rich, it
was a way of life. Mark, Kathleen, Leslie and Janet — they
worked together, played together, and loved together, all behind exclusive gates of the *Carlton Club*.

Available wherever paperbacks are sold, or order direct from the
Publisher. Send cover price plus 50¢ per copy for mailing and han-
dling to Penguin USA, P.O. Box 999, c/o Dept. 17109, Bergen-
field, NJ 07621. Residents of New York and Tennessee must
include sales tax. DO NOT SEND CASH.